HUSH

A GRIPPING SMALL TOWN THRILLER

CAREY BALDWIN

LOWMAN PRESS

For my mother and father
I love you.

PROLOGUE
SIX YEARS AGO

Near Tangleheart, Texas: Saturday, 6:00 P.M.

CHARLIE DREXLER NEVER hit a woman in his life—never had, never would. But he'd hurt Megan O'Neal just the same as if he'd blacked her eye. His throat closed up and his hands balled into fists when he recalled Megan's tears. The thought of a woman crying couldn't help but trigger gut-wrenching memories of Mom, crouched in the corner, hands covering her face... and Dad, standing over her, saying words like *sorry* and *never again* and *you're my world*.

Shadowboxing the wind, Charlie threw a right hook that connected with nothing, and then turned his face to heaven. Raindrops sprayed his skin like warm sweat shaken from a weary opponent. The woods outside Tangleheart were the closest thing the great state of Texas had to a rainforest, and the ground beneath his boots slurped and belched as he hiked up the dirt road that led to Megan's place. He'd parked a ways back because he knew from experience that if this drizzle turned into a summer storm, it'd be hell *and* high water getting his El Camino out. Farm Road 99 could turn to soup quicker than a Cup O' Noodles.

He punched the wind hard enough to spin himself around, and his fist slid through scorched air laden with moisture, portending a storm about to break wide open. From his new vantage point, he spotted Anna Kincaid, picking her way down a rocky trail that led from her father's hunting cabin to the road. He bent over, rested his hands on his knees and let out a groan. *Not Anna. Not now.*

Anna reached the road, and he doubled back to meet her. He didn't like her being out here alone, especially not with a big storm approaching, and he certainly couldn't take her up to Megan's with him. "Go home, Peaches."

Her chin came up in that proud way she had, and her voice carried a stubborn tone, in contrast to its inherent softness. "Don't call me Peaches and don't worry, I'm not here to disturb your tryst with Megan."

The no-nonsense way she planted her hands on her hips suited her message, but it also thrust her chest forward. Her white cotton top, made transparent by the rain, clung to her round breasts, and it took no small amount of willpower to prevent his eyes from straying in that direction. "Megan and I broke up. Now please, *Anna,* just go home before the weather gets any worse."

With a coldness he didn't feel, he turned his back and stared in the direction of the dilapidated farmhouse Megan had moved into after her mother kicked her out. He should get going, but he couldn't just walk away from Anna any more than he could leave Megan sitting all alone up there with a bad case of the blues she'd caught, courtesy of him.

"I-I hadn't heard." Anna put her hand on his shoulder and just that single, innocent touch made him want to pull her close and hold her against his heart, make promises he couldn't keep. But he wouldn't do that. Not to Anna. Anna tempted him more than any other woman, but he'd known her since she was a scared, skinny kid. His job was to look out for her, not seduce her.

"You're on your way up to her place." Hesitation flicked across her face, and then she drew in a sharp breath. "Have you changed your mind about calling things off?"

He shook his head. Breaking up with Megan had been the right thing to do, and even if he had a rewind button, he wouldn't press it. No matter how many times Megan said she loved him, no matter if he really had ripped her heart out—like she'd growled at him through clenched teeth—he didn't regret his decision. It was over between them. "No. It's only that she took it harder than I expected."

It'd stunned him how hard.

After all, he'd been gone the better part of the summer, working as a roustabout on the oil rigs off the coast of Corpus Christi. Before he'd left town, they'd promised to write to each other every day. But the twelve-hour days on the rigs left him too bone-weary to keep his promise. Seemed most times he managed to keep his eyes open long enough to take pen in hand, he wound up composing a letter to Anna instead of to Megan, and then he'd crumple that letter up and use it for practice shots into the trash basket. Megan hadn't kept her end up either, though, and he'd started to worry she was seeing someone else. That had wounded his pride. But it was only a flesh wound, and before he knew it, he'd actually begun to hope Megan had strayed.

"I accused her of cheating on me." He studied his boots, still feeling the knot of guilt in his chest that came from knowing he'd hurt a woman out of carelessness. "I'm one grade-A asshole for thinking she'd lie." His gaze met Anna's and held. "And for not loving her back the way she deserves."

"You can't choose who you love, Charlie." Anna pushed a

hank of blonde hair behind her ear and lowered her true-blue eyes.

He took the opportunity to memorize the way she looked: her damp skin glowing from the last rays of the setting sun, the shadow of her long lashes sweeping over her delicate features. While he was away, it was Anna's face he pictured each night before he fell asleep, and it was the thought of Anna walking around in the same world as him that made him want to get up each morning and start another backbreaking day.

"So, if you haven't changed your mind, then you've come to what...to apologize to Megan?" she asked, her voice near a whisper.

"No." He practically shouted the word. "Saying *I'm sorry* is not going to fix this mess." Then because this was Anna, because she was his best friend, and he'd always been able to say anything to her, he added, "My old man thinks *I'm sorry* and a bag of frozen peas for your cheek is the same as a get-out-of-jail-free card—one you can use however many times you like." A grimace pulled his cheeks so tight he could feel the wind across his teeth. "A man should take responsibility for the things he does."

Pulling up his shoulders, he swore to himself he'd never be like his father. If he wronged someone, no matter how small the infraction, he'd own up to it. He'd never take a get out-of-jail-free card—not even if Carrie Underwood herself presented it to him plastered onto an ice-cold bottle of Dos Equis. "I'm not here to say empty words. I'm here to make sure Megan's okay. Which is why you can't go up there with me, and I'm sure you can see the reason why."

Anna shook her head. "No. I don't see. I can be there for Megan, too. It's not as if she could be jealous of you and me—of our friendship. You've said it often enough: I'm just a kid who's been traipsing after you since grade school."

"Sorry, I only meant…" What? That had been a dick thing to say, and he knew it.

She gave him a tight smile.

Her shivering bottom lip begged him to pull her into his arms and replace the bitter taste of his cruel words with the sweetness of a kiss. Instead, he bit his tongue, a fitting punishment for the stupid things he'd said. Placing his hands on her shoulders, he dragged her near. His head bent to hers. His body shook from the effort of not kissing her. Then, with the palm of his hand, he cupped her cheek. "My Anna," he whispered.

As if his touch had blistered her skin, she jerked away. "Like I said, I'm not here to interfere with you and Megan."

His back stiffened at her response. Then his brain kicked in. There was a reason Anna was on her way to Megan's, and that reason had nothing to do with him. "So, why *are* you here?"

"Simone called. The cell reception was so bad all I could hear was static and something like *Megan's place. Please come.*"

"Why didn't you say so before?"

Pointedly, she arched one brow. "Because I was listening to you." And then she smiled, this time a real smile. *Thank God.* When Anna smiled, he thought there was no problem in the world they couldn't solve together. This was going to be a tricky situation, though, having Anna in the room while he comforted Megan. But he couldn't very well stop Anna from coming along if she'd been invited. *He* hadn't actually been invited. And Anna's sister, Simone, was a silver lining. If Simone was with Megan, that meant Megan hadn't been sitting up there in that run-down farmhouse, miserable and alone.

"Let's roll," he said, relief lightening his mood.

As he and Anna headed up the road, he pulled his miniature Maglite from his jeans pocket, twisted the top to turn it on and adjust the circumference of the beam. Stepping carefully, he concentrated on crisscrossing the light to illuminate Anna's path so she could avoid rocks and gullies.

He didn't see the cop car in Megan's drive until he was almost on top of it.

He didn't see the deputy until he came huffing toward them, one hand on a holstered gun.

A dirty, metallic scent mingled with the woodsy smell of rain in the air.

"Stay back, kids." The deputy patted his holster in a gesture that spoke volumes.

Charlie's pulse ratcheted up, sounding a drumroll in his ears.

This wasn't right.

He took a slow breath and tried to make sense of it all. The stench in the air was foreboding. Lights were on in the house, but it was eerily quiet. He only heard the scratching of the wind in the trees and the soft patter of rain falling to the ground. No stereo blaring, no conversation drifting from inside the house.

He took a measured step forward.

The deputy removed his hat, and water poured off the brim and down his pant leg, but the man didn't seem to notice. "Stay right where you are, boy. You can't go up there."

Like hell.

Charlie fired a *stay-back* look at Anna, and then darted around the deputy, but the officer grabbed his T-shirt and shoved him against the side of the car. As a searing pain cut straight up his back, he heard it—a soft cry from inside the cop car. In a burst of hope, he called out to her. "Megan!"

The window of the cruiser rolled down a few inches, and his hope disappeared. It was Anna's sister, Simone, sitting inside the car, sobbing into her hands. The damp air acted like glue in his lungs, sticking them together, making it hard to breathe, but somehow he managed to push out the question that had been gnawing a hole in his gut from the moment he'd seen the police cruiser in the drive. "Megan okay?"

Simone sputtered the words out in teary pieces punctuated with little gulps of air. "I'm. The one. Who found her."

"Found her?" The ominous phrase echoed in the wind. His face and hands went numb.

"You…Charlie… You got here too late."

1

PRESENT DAY

Tangleheart: Saturday, 6:00 P.M.

Anna Kincaid was the turned-down page corner in the book of Charlie Drexler's life. With a placeholder like Anna, he had to question his decision to skip ahead in the first place. Even setting aside their firefly nights of long ago, the sight of Anna making her way across the summer grass, deftly balancing a tray of—yes sir, those were deviled eggs all right—would still have knocked the wind out of him.

Dream girl walking.

Tonight, the corn-silk hair she'd crimped as a teen whipped long and naturally straight behind her, maybe because straight hair was the current fashion, or maybe because she'd finally realized she was goddamn beautiful in her own right. A simple sundress with spaghetti straps slipping off her bronzed shoulders conjured sensuality from innocence, and the curve of her hips, backlit by the setting sun, prompted a shameless reminder from his dick that he was a man who'd been without a woman for far too long. But his dick was the least of his problems. The real trouble was the way his heart kicked up when the familiar scent of her vanilla soap reached him.

Eschewing the vanity of perfume, Anna had always opted for natural fragrances and handmade soaps. To his way of thinking, her fancy soaps might be a natural, organic vanity, but they were vanity all the same. Yet year after year, he'd bitten back the urge to point out the flaw in her logic simply because he flat-out loved the way she smelled.

The way she smelled.

The way she shook back her hair when she laughed.

The way she moved.

But unlike times past, today he wasn't the only one admiring Anna. An overfed blue jay pecking the corncob bait on the Carlisle front porch paused to crane its neck and jabber a compliment as, with downcast eyes, Anna sideways-climbed the tricky steps. On second thought, maybe it wasn't the steps that were tricky. Maybe it was balancing those eggs while wearing high heels. High heels that showed off a pair of amazing calves. All he really knew was that he wanted Anna to look up. And when she saw him, he *needed* her to smile.

With his heart thundering in his ears, he waited for the moment of truth. He dragged a hand through his hair. He'd been scared plenty of times during his tour in Afghanistan, but he didn't recall his palms ever sweating like this. Anna climbed from the top step onto the porch, looked up and stopped dead in her tracks.

Helpless to contain the excitement welling inside him, he grinned—quite possibly beamed—at her. Anna's mouth, on the other hand, didn't roll out of its peppermint-pink bow. Her ridiculously blue eyes didn't crinkle at the edges, and she didn't offer so much as a glimmer of the smile that had woven its way into the very fabric of his dreams. If she had, he might never have recovered the sense to speak. "Hello, Peaches."

"Charlie."

His worst fear had been that the Anna of his boyhood would

tromp up the steps and rage at him, and he'd prepared himself for the worst. Or so he'd thought. What he hadn't prepared himself for was this. This neutral look on her face. This indifferent demeanor. It was as if Anna simply didn't care one way or another that he'd returned to her, determined to find out what he'd missed. It was as if the girl who'd looked up to him, who'd —let's face it—*worshiped* him, didn't care one way or another that he'd come home.

His chest deflated...briefly. But he was never one to stay down for the count. "Care to dance?" He grabbed her by the hand, pulled it high above her head and twirled her beneath his arm.

"Damn it, Charlie," she muttered as they both lunged for the plate of deviled eggs.

Triumphantly, he held out the rescued dish. "No harm done."

"To the eggs." She arched a matter-of-fact brow and made a quick survey of each high heel.

He set down the plate on the porch swing and moved in close. One hand found her hip while the other grazed her palm, and magically her arm rose with his. Her body canted forward until he could feel the brush of her warm breasts against his chest. Her knees buckled ever so slightly as he pulled her against him. She was trembling at first, but then she steadied. Her heart beat against him, keeping time with his own, and their breathing synchronized—as if their bodies knew how to talk to each other even if they didn't.

He swallowed hard. *Man up, Charlie.*

She shifted positions, bringing her hips in line with his, and by now, at least one part of him needed an admonishment to *man down*. "About that dance."

Sliding out of his arms, she quickstepped back, almost tumbling off the steps in the process. She skirted him, retrieved the platter off the porch swing and stuck it in his hands. "Welcome home, Charlie. The eggs are for you."

"You remembered."

Her nose scrunched up. "What?"

"Deviled eggs are my favorite."

"Are they?"

"C'mon, Peaches, don't be mad."

"Stop calling me Peaches. Mad about what?" she asked, her tone devoid of interest.

He squinted at her. She squinted back with no trace of animosity. Surely she wasn't going to let him off the hook that easily. He refused to accept this display of equanimity as truth. She was either mad and covering it up by playing it cool, or she had amnesia, and amnesia was the least likely explanation for her behavior he could think of. "Look, *Anna*, can we go somewhere private and talk?"

Shaking her head so hard her hair snapped against her cheek, she said, "No way."

"Why not?"

"First, it would be rude to disappear from your welcome home party. Simone has been planning this ever since your feet hit dirt in Tangleheart. Second, the eggs were Simone's idea, not mine, and third—"

She might've disabled his hands by sticking him with the platter of eggs, but he was far from disarmed. After all, he was carrying a backup weapon. In less than a heartbeat, he'd loaded up the trusty charm gun. *"Hey, girl."* He aimed a smoky look her way, one that could have felled hundreds, maybe thousands of librarians in a single shot.

Her eyes widened in surprise. "*Hey, girl?* Are you supposed to be Ryan Gosling in this scenario? Since when do you follow Ryan Gosling memes?"

"Since I saw your Facebook page."

Her lips transformed into a defiant pucker that reminded him of the time he watched her take her first shot of tequila. "You checked out my Facebook?"

"Guilty as charged. You're not the girl next door anymore, Anna. You're the hot librarian."

Her eyes flashed with determination, but he was confident of his impending victory. Anna's *you-cannot-make-me-smile* glare was a sure sign he could.

He cocked the charm gun. "*Hey, girl.* When's amnesty day at the library?"

No response.

Undaunted, he pulled the trigger. "'Cause I need to turn in an apology, and it's six years overdue."

Her puckered lips twitched at the edges. *Wait for it...ha!* Like a field of prickly poppies answering the call of the morning sun, her expression opened and transformed into a thing of beauty— the best smile he'd seen since the day he'd left Tangleheart, Texas.

"Six *and a half* years if you want to be accurate." He could hear that incredible smile creeping into her voice too.

"So you did miss me." He made an expansive gesture with his hands and tried not to sound cocky. "I mean, you seem to know exactly how long I've been away."

Her face flushed, and her mouth flatlined. "I'm just pointing out the facts, Charlie. No apology is necessary. I don't mean to sound harsh, but I think the past belongs in the past."

"Then let's go someplace private and talk about the future."

"You've got more nerve than sense, Charlie."

"And you've got great legs."

"I run."

His gaze crawled greedily from her well-turned calves, up and around her curves, climbing higher and higher until at last it reached her face and landed on her baby-blues. "It shows."

"Guess running's my own form of therapy, so I won't be needing your apology, Charlie. I'm over it."

"But maybe *I'm* not over it." After a six-year absence, he hadn't exactly planned on ambushing her on the front porch with his untidy, unresolved emotions, but he wasn't here to play tiddlywinks either. He'd come back to Tangleheart for two reasons, and Anna was one of them.

Anna tilted her head, surveying him closely. When her gaze reached his face, it lingered on his right cheek, where shrapnel had left a faint scar in the pattern of a starburst. "You've changed," she said, a soft catch in her voice.

"The Army does that to a man." As he lifted his chin, a torrent of memories tightened his jaw and made his heart tumble in his chest. He had, in fact, changed a great deal, and not just on the outside. The question was, had he changed enough to convince Anna to give him a second chance? Had he changed enough to *deserve* that chance?

Anna cleared her throat, like she had more to say but thought better of it. For an instant, he thought he saw tears in her eyes, but then she looked away, and with her hair floating behind her, blew past him so fast he didn't even have time to grab the door for her. He let loose a rough sigh. He didn't know much about what Anna Kincaid had been up to all these years, but one thing was certain: fantasizing about getting Charlie Drexler naked wasn't it.

Don't look back. Trying to make her mind a blank slate, Anna Kincaid whisked inside the front door and headed straight for the Carlisle kitchen. She did not wish to speak ill of the dead, nor did she wish to *think* ill of the dead, which was why she'd made a conscious effort all these years not to think about Megan

O'Neal. And Anna had stuck fast to her just-don't-think-about-it plan until this very evening, when Charlie Drexler had shown up on her sister's front porch, twirled her beneath his arm and turned her heart back six years.

Tonight, when he'd pulled her close, even the knee-buckling feel of his solid chest against her cheek couldn't stop her mind from churning through the murkiest part of their past. It couldn't stop her from thinking ill of a poor dead girl who'd deserved far more from life than she'd ever been given. But if it hadn't been for Megan O'Neal, Charlie wouldn't have enlisted in the Army straight out of high school, and he wouldn't have been part of that convoy when a suicide bomber tried to take out his entire squad. When Megan decided to end it all, she hadn't just taken her own life—she'd very nearly cost Charlie his too.

That terrible thought froze Anna's heart. She shook out her hands to relieve her tingling fingers.

Enough.

She'd meant it when she'd told Charlie the past belonged in the past.

Now, on the other hand, was the time to mentally prepare herself for an evening with her big sister, Simone. Smoothing her skirt, she glanced around the farmhouse kitchen. Farmhouse, of course, was Simone-speak for one of the most well-appointed homes in Tangleheart. Set on a one-hundred-acre spread of forested hills, this farm could boast no crops other than the stories Nate Carlisle liked to spin of their simple, country life.

Seeing the table in the nook set for four—five if you counted the high chair—Anna quickly realized that no other guests were coming to dinner. She'd been had by her big sister, which really should've come as no surprise. Simone's welcome home *party* was nothing more than a thinly veiled ploy to shove Anna and

Charlie together. She sniffed. At least the house smelled like her favorite homemade cinnamon rolls.

As her sister turned from the sink to greet her, Anna queued up her best stay-out-of-my-business voice. "Thanks for setting me up, Simone."

"Oh, you're welcome," Simone replied, either not catching or choosing not to understand Anna's subtext. "Thanks for bringing the appetizer. I hate the way deviling the eggs stinks up the house."

Anna waited a beat. *How long would it take for her sister to start in on her?* Simone's criticisms were always well-intentioned, but that did little to take the sting out of them.

"Where are the eggs, anyway?"

"I gave them to—"

"Oh, dear, Anna, put some makeup on before dinner, would you? You can borrow mine." Simone scurried about, fussing with the centerpiece. "You know I'm your biggest fan, but you're going to have to make an effort to look your best if you want to rope that man. Drex is far too handsome, and he has far too many prospects. A plain Jane won't do for the future Doctor Drex."

Most everyone, except Anna, called Charlie "Drex." In high school, she'd tried using the nickname a few times, but he'd put a fast stop to it.

I like it when you call me Charlie.

That's what he'd said, and somehow it had made her heart expand in her chest.

"I'm not interested in *roping* Charlie, as you put it, but in case you haven't noticed, I'm wearing both lip gloss and mascara."

"Oh, well, all right then. Very pretty indeed. And of course you're not after Drex. You're perfectly content to sit behind that desk at the library with your nose in a book. I always say you're very independent, and I'm sure you'll be just fine, even if you wind up a spinster."

Gnawing her lower lip, Anna tasted cherry gloss. Since forever, she'd endured Simone's digs with a smile on her face. After all, she'd caused Simone a great deal of embarrassment during their youth. In a small town like Tangleheart, your sister's sins were your sins, and the bullies hadn't been content with teasing only Anna—*the freak who didn't speak*. They'd gone after Simone almost as viciously as they'd gone after her, just because they were related.

But at this particular moment, it required so much effort not to focus on the fact that Charlie Drexler was in the next room, reliving the good old days with his buddy Nate that Anna simply couldn't summon the energy to be the bigger person and let Simone's barbs roll off her shoulders. "I'm twenty-five years old, Simone. That hardly puts me in spinster territory. Besides, the term spinster isn't exactly relevant to this century."

"Figure of speech." Simone waved her hand in the air. "I'm only looking out for you, you know."

She did know. Simone always stuck up for her, even when it'd meant not getting a spot on the cheer squad or an invitation to prom. Simone had sacrificed the popularity afforded a beautiful girl in a small town in order to take Anna's tormentors down a notch. And no doubt Anna would still be that odd girl out, that *freak* who only spoke in a whisper, if Simone hadn't invented a special talking game. Simone's game employed mountains of lemon drops and even more hugs to get Anna to speak up. It took years of Simone's ministrations before Anna finally learned to make herself heard.

No. There wasn't an unkind bone in Simone's five-foot-nine, Pilates-toned, post-baby body. Regretting her impatience, Anna said, "I know you've got my back, sis."

"I suppose you blame me for setting this trap. But the truth is I'm a better hostess than that."

Tonight, Simone's naturally pale skin appeared all but translucent against her flaming red hair, and her full lips were colorless beneath a sparkled gloss. An emerald-green silk tunic hung loosely over her slender arms.

"I asked Drex to come up with the guest list," Simone continued.

Anna touched her palm to her cheek and held in a sigh. "And?"

"You're it." Simone's delicate fingers jangled a charm bracelet. A sentimental smile played across her lips, and then faded. "You're not really mad at me, are you?"

When she threw her arms around her sister and squeezed, her breath caught at how thin Simone was, despite having given birth a mere ten months ago. "I could never *stay* mad at you. Especially not when you've got cinnamon rolls in the oven."

"My diabolical plan is working then." The chipper note in Simone's voice sounded forced.

Anna noticed a bleary look about her sister's eyes. But if something was wrong, Simone hadn't told her. Maybe Bobby was teething again. "Are you getting enough sleep?"

Simone just sighed.

"I think you should eat more and exercise less." Anna smiled to soften her words. "You look like you're one downward-facing dog away from the boneyard."

Dropping her chin, Simone glanced away, as if she didn't get the drift, even though Anna knew Simone understood her meaning perfectly well.

Apparently, humor wasn't working. Anna decided to take a more direct approach. "Everything good with you and Nate?"

On a long sigh, Simone reached in her pocket and pulled out

a letter-sized envelope. "This came in the mail today. It's a woman's handwriting. I just know it."

Anna looked at the envelope, addressed to Nate. The handwriting did appear feminine, but there was no return address to verify that. Her sister had always suffered a miserable jealous streak where Nate was concerned. Simone was hyperaware of the fact that she was several years older than Nate, and her insecurities had only worsened since Bobby had been born.

"Don't open that," Anna advised.

"Why shouldn't I?"

"Because none of your suspicions have ever been true. Because trust in a marriage works both ways, and your husband has a right to trust that you won't open his mail. If you want to know what's in that letter, just give it to Nate, and the two of you can open it together."

"But..."

"But nothing. You have a baby now, and you can't let jealousy ruin your marriage. Open the letter together. I'm sure it's nothing."

"I suppose you're right." Worry lines appeared around her sister's eyes.

"Smells like my wife's keeping a secret." Nate's good-natured baritone bellowed down the hall, growing louder and closer with every word.

Simone slipped the letter back in her pocket just as Nate and Charlie entered the open-style kitchen and family room.

"I never get baked goods unless a very expensive bomb's about to drop on me. You hiding a Neiman Marcus bill in your pocket, babe?" Although in reality Nate indulged his wife's every whim, he liked to toss around the clichés of a wears-the-pants husband in public. As he'd once eloquently explained it to Anna: *Nobody wants to get his sorry ass kicked out of the man club.*

In Anna's opinion, it was quite unlikely Big Nate, a six-foot-four tower of former linebacker muscle, would ever be kicked out of the Tangleheart man club. In Tangleheart, if a guy could play football, it didn't matter if his daddy was a rich SOB like Nate's, or a poor SOB like Charlie's. In Tangleheart, if a guy could play football, nobody cared about the rest of his résumé.

With a slight limp, a remnant of the blown-out knee that had ended his brief but glorious career in pro ball, Nate crossed to his wife and lifted her hand to his lips. "You look beautiful tonight, babe."

Pointedly, Charlie looked at Anna. "You *both* look beautiful tonight."

And just like that, Anna melted into a warm, mushy puddle—as if she were the last remaining bit of wax giving up the ghost beneath a flickering candlewick. Charlie looked as devastating as ever, his smoldering blue eyes providing a dramatic contrast to his thick, dark lashes and black hair. As always, his twice-broken nose made her want to reach out her hand to him in case he needed something to hold on to. Noticing her hand extending now, she whipped it behind her back.

How unfair that, after all this time, Charlie could show up out of nowhere and with merely a twirl, a corny librarian joke, and a deep-voiced compliment, stir up all her old yearnings. Straightening her spine, she waited for her breathing to return to normal. "Thanks. You men look good too…not as good as Simone and me, but good."

"I couldn't agree more." Nate watched Simone with a mix of adoration and fun in his eyes. "And I don't care how much money my sexy wife spends at Neiman's. I'm a happily married man, and…aw, hell…I don't care who knows it." Stepping close to Simone, he patted his pocket. "Go ahead, honey—reach right in and see what I've got for you."

Simone eagerly dipped her hand in her husband's pants pocket.

"Whoa. Not that far in my pocket."

Blushing, Simone pulled her hand out and along with it a flat, silver box imprinted with the Haltom's Jewelers logo. She smoothed back her hair, smiled happily and opened the box. She gasped, and then held up the contents: a square-cut emerald surrounded by a border of pavé diamonds, threaded on a delicate gold chain.

"Oh my goodness, Nate, you really shouldn't have." She turned her back so Nate could do the clasp on the necklace.

"I certainly should have. You're the mother of my little Bobby and the love of my life, aren't you?"

"Oh, no!"

"What's the matter, babe? You wear that phony emerald all the time, and I wanted you to have the real thing. But if you don't like this, I can take it back."

"No, I...I adore it, Nate." She reached for Nate's hand and squeezed it. "You're so thoughtful. I...I don't deserve you."

"Are you trembling from happiness then?"

Simone shook her head and pointed to the flat-screen television, which was on in the family room and set to mute.

Beneath a smiling photograph of a beautiful young woman a caption scrolled: *Channel Eight reporter, Catherine Timmons, found dead from a gunshot wound to the head. An apparent suicide. Details at ten.*

2

Tangleheart: Sunday, 10:00 A.M.

Charlie braced his shoulders and drew a breath of warm, humid air, made sweet by the multitudes of roses flanking the O'Neal front porch.

He'd come back to Tangleheart for two reasons. Reconnecting with Anna Kincaid was one of them. Finding and facing the truth about what had happened to Megan O'Neal was the other.

He pressed Maureen O'Neal's doorbell, and a jarring version of "The Yellow Rose of Texas" chimed out its fanfare. The house had coasted downhill since the last time he'd seen it. With the dirty pink paint peeling like a bad sunburn, and the tattered curtains in the windows drawn and faded yellow, the place gave off a *what's-the-use-anyway* vibe—except for one thing. Mrs. O'Neal's prize-winning rosebushes were as carefully tended as ever.

Good for her.

Apparently, Megan's mother understood the importance of holding tight to those things that bring us happiness in life. After Megan's suicide, he had run too fast and too far to consider what gave his own life meaning. It had taken a stint in the Army and years of therapy for him to figure out what really mattered to him. Picturing Anna's smile, he pressed the bell again.

He owed it to Mrs. O'Neal to pay her his respects, regardless of how much time had gone by, and then there was the matter of the note. Whether Megan's suicide note condemned him or absolved him of blame, he needed to know what was in it.

Out of his peripheral vision, he saw a curtain move. It might've been a cat, but... "Mrs. O'Neal." He called out loud and clear so she'd know it wasn't a Jehovah's Witness or a magazine salesman. "It's me. Charlie Drexler." Although he didn't expect she'd be pleased to see him, he hoped Megan's mother would at least be willing to speak with him.

The front door cracked open, and the morning sun illuminated a sliver of a woman's face floating in a sea of dust motes.

Shading her eyes, Mrs. O'Neal squinted and eased the door open another inch or two. "Drex? Is that you?"

"Yes ma'am. It's me. I don't mean to disturb you, but I was hoping we could talk about Megan."

"Hush." She hissed the word. Her body began to tremble, her knees creaked as if they might buckle, and then with surprisingly strong hands, she reached out, gripped his collar and yanked him inside. Maureen O'Neal poked her head out the door and scanned the perimeter of her yard before shoving the door closed behind him and sagging against the wall. "You weren't followed, were you?"

"Followed?" Maybe she'd gone a little *eccentric* after Megan died. She wouldn't be the first parent grief had driven around the bend.

"Tailed." Straightening, she knotted the belt on her ratty blue bathrobe. She pulled a pack of Lucky Strikes from her pocket and tapped it against the butt of her hand. Inside, the house smelled stale, like cigarettes...and booze. Maybe the booze explained her odd behavior.

"I wasn't followed. I mean, not that I know of." When he took a step toward her, his shin bumped a box that clattered like a bunch of dinner plates. As it turned out, *Plates* was scrawled on the cardboard flap in marker. *Score one for his detective skills.* Once his eyes adjusted to the dimness inside the house, he noted other boxes scattered about the room—and a half-empty bottle of Jack Daniels on the coffee table. "You're moving."

"Disappearing is more like it." A cigarette now jittered between her fingers. She struck a match and puffed until the tip of her cigarette glowed. Orange light flared across a set of deep lines that carved her upper lip. The Mrs. O'Neal he remembered had been a looker—in a flashy, rodeo-queen sort of way. Today, wearing a haggard expression, her hair cut in a short bob, the gray allowed to streak through her auburn hair at will, she seemed much older than her forty-something years. She wore no makeup, and her once saucy blue eyes had gone flat. He didn't detect a trace of the sass-to-the-max woman she'd been while Megan lived.

The weight of his guilt suddenly crashed down on him. The words he'd rehearsed on the way over seemed stiff, but he didn't know how else to proceed. "Let me say, first of all, how very sorry I am for your loss...and for my part in it. I don't expect you to forgive me, but I hope you know I'll never stop regretting the pain I caused Megan and you." He released a long breath and felt his chest contract and then expand more easily than before.

She took another shaky drag off her Lucky. "I'm the one who should be apologizing to you."

In response to this incomprehensible remark, his chin snapped back. His mind went completely blank, and then scrambled to make sense of her words. Apparently Mrs. O'Neal had been carrying around some guilt of her own. He grasped at the first possibility that occurred to him. "You don't owe me an apology or anything at all, but if you've been blaming yourself because you kicked Megan out of the house…"

"What are you talking about, son?" She walked to the coffee table, ground out her cigarette in a chipped ceramic ashtray, and poured a slug of Jack into a plastic cup. "I never kicked Megan out of this house."

"Why would she say you did?"

"Same reason she told all her fibs, I suppose. Megan craved attention." She tossed back the whiskey and coughed. "Did you know I had her when I was only sixteen? I weren't a perfect mother, but I did my best. You want a drink?"

It was a little after ten o'clock in the morning. "Yeah. A drink would be good."

He waited while she went into the kitchen and came back with another plastic cup.

Her eyes no longer had that flat, glassy look. Instead, they pleaded with him for understanding. "I didn't kick Megan out of the house. She left in a huff because she didn't want to follow my rules about boys and drinking." Mrs. O'Neal splashed whiskey into both cups and handed one to him. "I couldn't set an example, so I set rules instead. I wanted her to have a better life than me." Her voice cracked. "Maybe I was harder on her than I should've been."

"Megan loved you," he said, not really knowing, but hoping it was true.

"And she sure liked you a lot, son. It weren't all pretend." One hand went to her collarbone and swept back and forth, searching. "Megan wore that necklace you gave her every day, right up to the end. You remember the one? It had an old-fashioned key dangling off it."

"The key to my heart." At least that's what he'd told Megan. Megan had never truly had possession of his heart, but he did work hard on that damn necklace. Took him a full week of shop class, and she had smiled so brightly when he'd given it to her. *No one ever made me a necklace before, Drex.* She'd tiptoed up and kissed his cheek. Nostalgia clogged his throat. "I'd like to see it. I mean, if you still have it."

Her brow drew down in a deep frown. "I wanted to bury that necklace with my baby, she loved it so, but after she died, it weren't nowhere to be found." Her shoulders drooped. "Look, Drex. You've said your piece. Thank you for caring about my girl. But none of this was your doing. So you can go on home now...and please don't tell anyone you were here."

She went to the window and peeked out, quickly letting the curtain fall back in place before turning to face him again.

Clearly, she was anxious for him to go, but he hadn't finished his business here. His gaze met hers. "I hate to put you through anything else, but there's something I need to ask."

Just as Mrs. O'Neal had done, he lifted the cup to his lips and belted the whiskey. It singed his throat on the way down, and he was glad of it. "It's about the note. If you could just tell me what was in Megan's suicide note, it would help me put the past behind me once and for all."

Her hands covered her eyes. Her shoulders vibrated, and then she stumbled across the room and crumpled into a sloppy heap on the couch. "I guess you got the right to ask. But there weren't no note, Drex. That's one reason I went to Deputy Hawkins and asked him what made him so sure my baby did *that* to herself. How did he know Megan weren't murdered?"

"There was no note?" In all this time, he'd never considered that possibility.

"I thought that was suspicious, but Deputy Hawkins took me by the hand and explained that most people who kill themselves don't leave notes. Megan weren't murdered. So the fact there weren't no note didn't mean nothing."

His head pounded from the smoke and the whiskey. He picked up the bottle off the table and poured himself another drink. No note did mean something. It meant he'd never know for sure if Megan killed herself because he broke it off with her, or if she'd had some other reason.

Maureen continued to talk, as though the memories had come flooding back, and she couldn't dam them up any longer. "Anyway, I came home and I Googled up *suicide* and I found out what Hawkins told me was true. There's usually no note. But I found out something else while I was about it, and I went back to the deputy and told him I didn't think my baby shot herself in the head. Most girls use more ladylike methods, like pills and whatnot."

"That always bothered me too," he said, between swigs. But there had been no evidence of a robbery, and Megan had been in a terrible state of mind.

"Anyway, Hawkins got his back up. I didn't get the hand-holding treatment that time around so much as the brush-off. He said all the evidence pointed to suicide. There weren't no robbery. She had no known enemies. Megan's prints were the only ones on the gun. There was gunshot residue on Megan's hands."

She took a long draw off her cigarette, followed by another. "Then I called him a rotten liar."

"Why would you do that?"

Her fingers passed over her lips. "Because the night Megan died, Hawkins came here all keyed up, told me there weren't no gunpowder on Megan's hands. He asked me did I know someone who wanted to hurt her. And then just two days later, he looks me square in the eyes and says he made a mistake, his test was wrong and the crime lab's test was right. He's sorry, he says, but there *was* gunpowder on Megan's hand after all. There had to be, he says, because electric microscopes don't lie."

Charlie didn't know much about forensics, but he was on a first-name basis with microscopes courtesy of his premed studies. "Did Hawkins maybe say *electron* microscopes don't lie?"

"That's it exactly. *Electric microscopes don't lie*. He told me to chin up to the stone-cold truth. My girl was heartbroke, and she shot herself and I had to accept it."

Hawkins was right—at least about electron microscopes. Those findings would be dead accurate, more so than any rapid test for gunshot residue the deputy might have done at the scene. Charlie needed to sit down.

Maureen began to slur her words. "I went home like he told me, but I couldn't sleep that night. So the next day, I went back to Hawkins, and I asked if anyone checked Simone Kincaid's hands for gunshot residue. That was before Simone was a Carlisle, you know."

He slumped down next to Mrs. O'Neal on the couch, her words drilling into him. She thought Simone might've killed Megan. Even for a grieving mother, that seemed like a stretch. Simone was a wonderful kid, with no motive at all for harming Megan—at least not any motive that Charlie could dream up.

"Hawkins laughed at me. He told me to go home and to stop watching those TV crime shows. And that's exactly what I did. I went home, and I convinced myself that it happened just like he said. I told myself Megan weren't scared of no intruders. She bought that revolver at the gun show because she didn't want to live anymore."

Mrs. O'Neal's shoulders pumped up and down like she was holding back a hard sob. "I accepted the explanation that the law gave. Megan's death was a suicide. And I kept the money because I needed it, and because I figured *he owed it to me*."

Charlie's eyebrows shot up. He turned and put his hands on her shoulders, both to comfort her and to help her stay focused. "What money? Who gave it to you?"

"Did I forget to mention the money?" She tapped her nose with her index finger. "Five hundred dollars. Came like clockwork every two weeks—until ten months ago, that is. Then it just stopped. Well, I figured if he didn't owe me nothing no more, I didn't owe him nothing no more. So I went to that reporter, and I told her I thought *he'd* been sending me money all those years just because he didn't want his good name bandied about in the same sentence with my poor girl."

It was all Charlie could do not to shake her. He tried to keep his voice low and easy. "Who didn't want his name bandied about?"

Mrs. O'Neal catapulted to her feet, and Charlie went with her. She pushed his hands off her shoulders and somehow managed to stay upright. "I won't tell you. I told Catherine Timmons and look what happened to her."

"Catherine Timmons?" A spider crawled down his back. Catherine Timmons—the reporter who, according to the news, shot herself in the head yesterday.

Mrs. O'Neal nodded, and her bright-red face turned pale pink.

No wonder she was nervous. "You think Catherine Timmons, the Channel Eight reporter, is dead because of something you said to her ten months ago?"

Her chin came up, and she stood perfectly straight. She seemed to have jolted herself into some sort of temporary sobriety. "I honest to God don't know. That's the worst part. I don't know for sure who sent me money the last six years or why. I don't know a damn thing about what happened to Megan in that farmhouse. I don't know if it was suicide, like I made myself believe all these years, or if it weren't."

She buried her face in her hands, and when she looked back up, her eyes flooded with tears. "I don't know if that reporter copied Megan and shot her own self in the head, or if someone else had a hand in it. But I do know this: the sheriff—Hawkins is the sheriff now, you know—the sheriff don't give a rat's ass, and I can't take no more chances. I'm getting out of this town, and I ain't never coming back."

She beat her fists against her chest. "I've owed you an apology, Drex, a long time. Now you have it."

"No. You've got that backward. I should've come here six years ago and told you how sorry I am for what happened. Instead, I ran away. I did nothing to comfort you. I didn't even stay in town long enough to go to Megan's funeral." He reached out and offered her his hands, palms up. "Why would you ever owe me, of all people, an apology?"

"Because you *do* give a rat's ass. You run off to war and all but got yourself killed on account of you felt responsible for what happened to my Megan." She took his hands. "And here this whole entire time *I knew* that while you were away working the oil rigs, Megan took up with someone else. *I knew* she got herself pregnant by that someone else, and then she lost *his* baby, and then she shot herself. But I never told you. And I never said a damn word about *him* after that because of five hundred lousy dollars every two weeks. That's why I owe you an apology."

His breath hitched. He opened his mouth to speak, but couldn't.

She gripped his hands harder. "You are *not* responsible for Megan's death. Don't ask me again who the other man was because I won't tell you. I'll be gone before dark, and I pray to God I never see Tangleheart, Texas, again."

3

Tangleheart: Monday, 6:00 P.M.

CHARLIE HAD SOUNDED odd on the phone—troubled. He'd said he needed to talk, and Anna had figured she had enough good sense to keep her emotions in check around him. But when she'd arrived at Charlie's apartment, he'd put his hand on the small of her back to guide her way, and his touch had triggered a dangerous yearning that started low in her belly and spread all the way up through her aching chest. Clearly, she'd overestimated her good sense. Coming here had been a mistake —a big one.

She started to remove her purse from her shoulder, and then thought better of it. "You said you wanted to talk to me about something."

He plopped down in the dead-middle of a small leather couch. His long legs opened wide, and then he patted a spot near his thigh. "Sit with me."

Her gaze darted about the living room, taking in the unadorned white walls and a clean but worn brown carpet. The laminated coffee table looked like the type you'd get at Rent-A-

Center. There were no chairs in the room, nor was there a loveseat to augment the couch. The place screamed temporary, and why wouldn't it? Charlie had just gotten into med school, at UT Austin. Classes started in the fall. Too bad she didn't know how to be his temporary friend. "I can't stay, so do you or don't you have something important to say to me?"

"How 'bout *I'm sorry*?"

"We've covered that. You apologized, quite charmingly I might add, just after spinning me around on Simone's front porch. And then I said there was no need for an apology, which in fact there is not, and that we should keep the past in the past. That was around forty-eight hours ago. Surely you haven't forgotten already."

"No. I haven't forgotten, and I was charming, I'll grant you that, but I didn't get to say sorry properly because you cut me off."

"So now I owe you the apology?"

"Peaches, just sit the hell down...please."

Wishing she'd kept her keys in hand, she started digging through her purse for them. *Way too much junk in there: receipts, candy, pennies.*

He patted that alluring spot next to him again. "If you really want to put the past behind us, then hear me out. Let me say what I need to say, and after that I won't bother you again...not unless you want me to."

Charlie Drexler *bothering* her. *How many of her teenage fantasies had revolved around that scenario?* She took a deep breath and managed to whisper, "Fair enough." She nudged Charlie's knees to the side so she could sit down without their bodies touching and then sank down on the couch.

"I'm *sorry*." He picked up her hand and stroked his thumb in circles over her palm, sending little sparks flying up her arm.

So much for not touching.

"When Megan died, I did exactly what I swore I'd never do. I took a get-out-of-jail-free card. Instead of staying here and dealing with the heartache I'd caused, I ran like hell."

To keep from interrupting him, she held her breath. Enlisting in the military and putting himself in harm's way for his country hardly seemed like playing a get-out-of-jail-free card to her.

A sharp line appeared between his eyebrows. "Of course, running away didn't work. The harder I tried to forget about Megan's death, the more it haunted me."

She let out her breath. Everywhere his thumb touched, sparks followed, but the sinking feeling in the pit of her stomach anchored her to reality. Each word he spoke made it increasingly clear that Megan's ghost stood between them. And if her ghost stood between them after all this time, no doubt it always would. "You're still not over Megan," she blurted. Apparently, as absolutely crackers as it seemed, she was jealous of a dead woman.

"Not true at all. I am over her, and I was over her. I broke up with her. Remember? At the time, I thought that was why she killed herself." His head tilted to the side. "Megan was seeing someone else. Did you know about that?"

Her hand stifled a sharp gasp, and then she stuttered, "W-what? Who?"

"You sure you don't know who Megan was seeing? I mean, in this town it's hard to keep anything secret." His eyes narrowed, as if he thought she might be lying to him.

Her head jerked up. "I've had just about enough of this, Charlie. I'm tired of talking about her. If I knew a damn thing about Megan and another man, I would've told you at the time. I would not, could not, have let you carry that guilt around with you. Now if you don't mind, I'm going to leave." To control the shiver in her voice, she kept it low. "And I'll be taking you up on your offer of not bothering me again—*ever*."

He stopped making thumb circles and slipped his fingers around her wrist like a manacle. She twisted her hand, tugging, trying to get free.

"Don't run away. It doesn't work. Trust me, I know from personal experience. I had to come back and face my demons." He hesitated. "And...Anna, I had to come back for you."

His words rang in her ears and echoed in her thoughts: *for you*.

It took her a beat to catch her breath. "Well, you took your sweet time about it, didn't you? I *loved* you, Charlie." She tried to blink away the stinging sensation in her eyes. "There, I said it. *I loved you*. And you left town without even saying good-bye. I had to hear it from Nate you'd run off to enlist."

"And I'm trying to tell you, trying to show you, how sorry I am. That's why I came home. I never should have left you without trying to make sense of what was happening between us, because the truth is I *knew* you loved me. But...surely you can see how overwhelming that felt under the circumstances."

Her mouth had gone to cotton, and she could hardly swallow. She didn't want to talk about this anymore. All she wanted was to go back to pretending that none of it mattered. Everything had been just fine right up until the moment Charlie showed up and started dredging up the past. With Simone's assistance, Anna had hired a night nurse to help with their father, and that had freed her to finally get her own place. She loved her job at the library, and Mrs. Marlowe had even arranged a special schedule so that Anna could take classes at a nearby community college. Then, ten months ago, she had become a doting and very happy aunt to little Bobby. Life was good, and she'd worked hard to make it that way.

The last thing she needed was Charlie coming around, saying sorry.

The last thing she needed was to remember all those horrible nights she'd lain sleepless in her bed, anguishing over the way he'd left and terrified he'd be killed in combat.

On a hard sigh, she said, "I get it. You knew I loved you. How stupid of me to think you'd be the only one in town who didn't. Naturally, you found the fact that I loved you overwhelming, and that's why you didn't bother to say good-bye. That's why I haven't had a word from you in six years even though I was supposed to be your best friend."

"I didn't write to you, Anna, because I wasn't *whole*." His face paled. With his free hand, he tilted her chin, forcing her to meet his eyes. "I know you've heard about that bomb that took out most of my squad, and I guess maybe it seems to you like everything should've become crystal-clear to me right then and there. They say your life flashes before your eyes, but it didn't happen that way for me. I was just so damn sad after...but I did know one thing: I'd been spared when others had died, and I had damn well better make my life count for something."

Her imprisoned hand had gone as numb as her heart. "So you decided to become a doctor."

"Yeah. After the Army, I went to college. And it wasn't until a couple of years ago, when my mom visited me at UT, and she told me she was leaving my old man, that I started going to a psychologist. At first I went with my mom, because she asked me to, but later, I kept going on my own. Anna, I had to be sure I wouldn't turn into the kind of man my father is. Until then, I couldn't even think of being in the kind of relationship that might turn into something real."

Her arm throbbed all the way to her elbow, and she could feel his pulse bounding against her wrist, hear the anguish in his voice.

"But that wasn't the only problem. Megan told me she loved me, and I couldn't love her back—not when all I ever thought about was you. I believed Megan killed herself because of me, and Megan was strong. Anna, you were so fragile. I couldn't risk hurting you. Don't you see that?"

Actually, she did. And that ought to have made everything better, only it didn't. She'd always known Charlie had been running from his guilt about Megan's suicide, no matter how misplaced that guilt had been. What she hadn't ever truly understood was why he'd left town without a word to her, his best friend. And then, the very worst thing ever: *six years of radio silence.*

Now she understood. Now she had closure. Well, closure was highly overrated. She didn't feel better at all. In fact, she wanted to spit and scream and yes, she wanted to cry. But that wasn't her style. She kept her voice soft, unrattled. "You think I'm fragile?"

Looking down at her wrist, he seemed to become aware of how tightly he gripped it and loosened his hold, but he didn't let her go. "I thought you were fragile at the time, yes. Think about your childhood, Anna. You barely even spoke until you were twelve years old."

"And you think I whispered because I'm fragile—weak?" Her voice became dangerously uncalm, and she wrenched her hand free from his grasp. "You don't have any idea how much willpower it took for me to stay silent."

The truth she'd never told anyone, not even her own sister, came rushing out. "I whispered because my old man told me that if I was quiet, if only I was a good little girl and didn't make noise when Daddy had a headache, my mommy would come back home. And I *believed* him. I poured him another drink, and then I shut my mouth. Even after Daddy took back everything he'd said, even after he dragged me to all those doctors and begged me to talk, I kept on whispering, because I wanted to believe I could make my mother come back home."

A harsh laugh shook her. "I'm not fragile, Charlie. Not in the least. What other little girl do you know who'd be strong enough to play the quiet game for five whole years?"

His eyes were fixed on her, unblinking. Thank God, she didn't see pity in them. Placing his hands on her shoulders, he drew her near. "I should've been there for you. You have every right to be angry, baby—with your mother, your father —with *me*."

"Angry?" Her throat closed around the word. Was it anger that fueled this hard heat inside her chest?

Charlie lifted his fingers and traced her lips. The blue blaze in his eyes smoldered into deep pewter. His touch was a balm, softening her heart, and somehow all that bubbling rage she hadn't owned before changed course, transforming itself into urgent, physical need. Suddenly, all she could feel was the white-hot ash of unfulfilled desire.

A dull thud sounded in her ears, and she recognized it as the noise of her purse falling to the floor. As Charlie's finger continued to scald a path across her lips, he opened his knees until his thigh touched hers. Her pulse rampaged all over her body. She'd wanted this man since the day she'd been old enough to recognize physical desire, and now, at least in this particular moment, he wanted her too. She drew a slow, determined breath—whatever happened between them tonight was going to be on *her* terms.

"I'm so sorry, Peaches…"

"Shut up, Charlie." She slipped her hand under his T-shirt, and the muscles in his abdomen bunched beneath her touch. His skin was hot and slick beneath her palms as she explored his chest, testing herself, unsure how far she wanted to take this.

He groaned, clearly wanting more. She crossed her legs to

ease the pressure building between her thighs. She wanted more too. Grasping the hem of his shirt, she yanked it over his head, tossed it aside and let her eyes linger on the cut muscles of his chest, and then drift to his jeans, where his ample desire was more than evident.

"I've dreamed of this. Of you, touching me this way." He breathed the heated words into her ear.

Drawing back, she watched his face darken with need. She slid her hands lower, sketching the long, hard shape of him.

"That's so nice, Anna." He half spoke, half groaned, before capturing her hands in his and pushing her back on the couch.

She caught his male scent as he came over her, and the weight of his body pressed her into the cushions. When he brushed rough, wet lips over the nape of her neck, thick pleasure poured through her, like honey through a comb, filling her hollow places, replacing what was empty with what was sweet.

She was too lost in that heavy sweetness to hear the door open, or the footsteps that must have followed. Charlie heard them though, because he bolted upright and threw his hand protectively across her. On her back, she opened her eyes and found herself staring into the dilated pupils of her brother-in-law.

Sweat poured from Nate's hairline, and his face was red and puffy. His breath stank of whiskey. It looked as though he'd run the distance from his place to Charlie's—but of course that was unlikely.

"I tried your house first, Anna. I thought I might find you here." Panting, Nate doubled over. "Have you...have you heard from Simone?"

She jerked to a sitting position and forced her breathing to slow. Charlie tried to wrap his arm around her. Instinctively, she pulled away. Every muscle in her body went taut and battle ready. "No. I haven't seen Simone. Not since yesterday. What is it, Nate? What's wrong?"

"S-something terrible. Simone never came home last night." His hands were shaking and his voice tore open in a sob. "Simone and Bobby are missing."

4

Tangleheart: Monday, 9:00 P.M.

SHERIFF HAWKINS HAD called a meeting at Nate and Simone's place and assembled all the *guests* in the family room. Hawkins instructed everyone to take a seat in a semicircle around the coffee table. As the sheriff paraded around, raising an eyebrow here, shooting a distrustful glance there, Charlie couldn't help but think the only thing necessary to complete the whole mystery-movie atmosphere was Colonel Mustard brandishing a candlestick. Hands were nervously stuffed into pockets, feet were shuffled, and brows were wiped. Tea was even served—by Jenny Jacoby.

Jenny, a student at the Tangleheart culinary school, boarded with Nate's parents, Caleb and Lila Carlisle, in exchange for cooking and cleaning. Sheriff Hawkins insisted Jenny attend the meeting because she was the last known person to see Simone and Bobby. Caleb Carlisle insisted, despite the sheriff's protests, that the young woman be put to use. So Jenny had made tea, and while Hawkins paced, she cheerfully poured fragrant liquid into flowery cups whose handles were far too small for Charlie's thumbs.

Then, at last, Jenny sat down on the couch next to Anna. Anna had seated herself next to Charlie—he considered that a good sign.

"Everyone got their tea?" The sheriff tossed a daggered glare at Caleb Carlisle, clearly displeased the older man had usurped his authority regarding the proceedings. "Good." He answered his own question, thwarting any further delay. "Then I'd like to retrace Simone Carlisle's steps on the day she went missing."

Charlie's legs had gone stiff, but he resisted the urge to get up and stretch. Hawkins seemed to need the advantage of being the only man standing in order to maintain control of the room.

Hawkins approached Anna. "You say you saw your sister around ten a.m. on Sunday. She was wearing her yellow Anne Klein jogging suit and black Nike tennis shoes. Is that right, Miss Kincaid?"

Anna's fingers clenched around her teacup. "Yes. She stopped by the library."

Charlie wished he could make this easier on her, but Anna probably wouldn't appreciate him putting his arm around her in public. He gave her knee a quick squeeze instead.

"Bobby with her?" Hawkins continued.

"He was dressed in a Texas Rangers baseball shirt and white shorts." Anna's cup clattered as she replaced it in the saucer. "I have a picture on my phone of Bobby wearing that outfit. Will that help?"

Hawkins scribbled into a notepad, ripped a paper out and handed it to Anna. "Send it to my e-mail, if you don't mind. What time did Simone leave the library on Sunday?"

"She was there about an hour, so I'd say eleven."

Caleb Carlisle bolted to his feet, bumping the coffee table and sloshing tea on the carpet. "Who cares if Simone took Bobby to the damn library? Why haven't you put out an Amber Alert?"

"We've been through that, Dad." Nate remained slumped on the couch, his chin boring a hole in his chest. His lips thinned into a worried line. "Bobby's with his mom."

Hawkins nodded. "By all accounts, Bobby is with his mother. And his mother has every legal right—"

"To run off with my grandson? Like hell she does." Carlisle's face sagged, and his eyes grew moist. A barely perceptible tremor had crept into his voice. "You've got to do something, Hawkins."

"I'm trying to do something, Caleb…sir. I'm trying to do my job." His tone held surprising resolve. "So how about you take your seat and let me get on with my questions."

Carlisle let out a resigned breath and sat down. As instructed. That had to be a first. Charlie might have underestimated Hawkins.

The sheriff next turned to Jenny Jacoby. "Miss Jacoby, you were at the home of Lila and Caleb Carlisle yesterday, Sunday, when Simone and Bobby stopped by. Approximately what time would that have been?"

"Noon."

"So Simone must have gone straight from the bank to her in-laws' place."

What?

"The bank?" Charlie and Anna asked in unison.

Hawkins put up his hand. "Simone withdrew her maximum daily allowable, five hundred dollars, from the Safeway ATM on Sunday at eleven thirty." He gave Jenny an encouraging smile. "Go on, Miss Jacoby."

"Lila—Mrs. Carlisle—was at her woman's club meeting, and I was making appetizers for a card party later that afternoon. I was surprised to see Simone at the door because she knows Mrs. Carlisle has her Red Hat Club every Sunday while Mr. Carlisle plays golf."

Hawkins grazed his hand over his close-cropped brown hair, preening for pretty Jenny Jacoby. "Maybe she forgot."

Jenny shrugged. "Anyway, she asked to come inside, even though the Carlisles weren't home. She said she needed to change Bobby's diaper. The weird thing is she didn't use any of the downstairs rooms. She went all the way upstairs, was gone a good twenty minutes, and when she came back down, she hadn't changed the baby."

"You don't know that." Anna rushed to her sister's defense, her voice shaking with fury.

Charlie grabbed her hand and held on. To hell with what people thought.

An apologetic look came over Jenny's face. "Simone's a good mom, Anna. But I could *smell* him...and that's when I noticed Simone didn't even bring a diaper bag inside. How could she have changed Bobby if she left his diaper bag in the car?"

Jenny's bright-green eyes seemed guileless, intelligent. Charlie didn't know her at all, but his instincts told him she was telling the truth. As strange as that truth seemed.

Nate still hadn't looked up. His father put an arm around him. It was one of only a handful of times Charlie had ever seen Caleb show his son any physical affection.

"Has anyone tried tracking her cell phone?" Jenny suggested softly.

"No luck," Hawkins responded. "She may have removed her battery from her phone. I'm sorry to say this, Nate, but it seems to me like Simone doesn't want to be found. Maybe all she needs is a cooling-off period."

Nate finally looked up. His eyes flicked around the room. "Why wouldn't my wife want to be found? Why would she need a cooling-off period? We haven't argued." His gaze landed on Anna. "No more than usual, at least."

Anna stood and went to her brother-in-law. She touched his shoulder in a show of support.

Nate placed his hand on top of Anna's, and then looked up to meet her eyes. "Did she tell you where she went, Anna? She must have told you something."

Anna drew in a sharp breath. Charlie could read the anguish in her eyes. "Of course not. I would never keep a secret like that."

Carlisle came to his feet again, a hard look on his face. "It's a fair question, Anna. Everyone in this town knows the Kincaid sisters always have each other's backs."

5

Tangleheart: Monday 11:30 P.M.

ABANDONING HER KEYS in the front door of the library, Anna flipped on the lights and sprinted for the security panel on the far wall. With only a moment to spare, her index finger connected with its target. Beeps sounded. Green lights flashed. The security system shut off without a hiccup. Triumphantly, she whirled, aiming two thumbs up at Charlie.

His response: the high arch of one amused eyebrow. "Your mission, should you decide to accept it, is to sneak into the Tangleheart Public Library, where you are, in fact, authorized to be at any time, and disarm the security system, which you, in fact, programmed yourself." He'd made his voice the rich velvet of a radio announcer, and now he was giving her an exaggerated slow clap. "Dangerous business, breaking into the library after hours."

She waved a dismissive hand, putting too much spin on her wrist and banged it against the wall. Her hand stung a little—so did Charlie's sarcasm. Joking around had always been Charlie's way, and she knew he was only trying to distract her from worry about Simone, but he didn't seem to understand how important her position at the library was to her. "Go ahead and make fun, but I could lose my job over this."

"Then Mrs. Marlowe must've changed. Last I heard, she was as addicted to the pleasure of your company as to that nip of brandy from the bottle she keeps hidden in her desk drawer. Does she still bring you brownies on Saturdays and call you *dearheart*?"

Nursing her wrist, she said, "I suppose you think protecting the privacy of a library patron is less important than doctor-patient privilege."

He shrugged. "I think you're okay on this one. The library patron in question happens to be your sister."

"This is serious stuff. Maybe Mrs. Marlowe wouldn't fire me if she found out, but I know I'm violating a professional code of ethics. If I didn't think Bobby and Simone might be…"—the tightness in her throat transformed her voice into a thin thread—"in real trouble, I'd never allow you in here. I'd never misuse my position as librarian to snoop into any patron's business, not even my sister's."

"You're right—I'm being a jerk."

He sounded sincere, but after that slow clap… She drew her bottom lip between her teeth, considering.

"No. I mean it. I know how hard this must be for you." His voice lowered, and his eyes lingered on her mouth in a way that made the room suddenly seem far too warm.

She released her lip from between her teeth. Her pulse still raced, even though the sprint from the door to the security panel was nothing compared to the hills she ran most weekends. Crossing her arms over her chest, she took a step back—just far enough to escape his force field.

Charlie continued to study her. His head angled sideways. "Remember the time we went to see *Knocked Up,* and there was no one manning the ticket booth?"

Knocked Up? Surely he wasn't still holding a grudge over twenty lousy dollars. "My stars, Charlie. Is there going to be a point to this little stroll down memory lane? Because we've got stuff to do here."

A nostalgic look preceded his words. "I wanted to go inside and catch the movie for free, but you insisted on chasing down the manager and paying for the tickets. I never thought I would say this, but I've missed that sort of thing about you."

She uncrossed her arms and planted her hands on her hips. "You stayed mad a whole week."

"Well, yeah. Your overdeveloped conscience cost me twenty bucks, but when you don't see someone for a long time, it's the little things that sneak up on you and make you realize..." His gaze went to a spot somewhere over her shoulder. "We should get on with it. I honest to God don't want to cause trouble for you with Mrs. Marlowe, and the sooner we figure out what Simone was looking for, the sooner we can start our search."

Our search. The knowledge that Simone and Bobby's fate might very well depend on them weighed heavily on her heart. Sheriff Hawkins believed Simone had left of her own volition, that she was nursing a jealous streak. He'd taken a missing persons report and put out a BOLO, but it had seemed to Anna as if he were just going through the motions. Convinced this was a routine domestic incident, Hawkins wasn't keen on calling out the cavalry just yet, but Anna knew enough to understand how important the first forty-eight hours were in missing person cases. If Bobby and Simone hadn't been found by then...

"Charlie." To keep the fear out of her voice, she paused and gulped air. "Thank you."

He took her hand and turned it over in his. "Sure. But for what?"

"For being here." She kept her hand in his, allowing herself to feel safe, if only for the space of a single heartbeat. "I don't know if I could do this without your help."

"I think you could do just about anything. But we do make a good team." As she pulled her hand free, his brow furrowed. "I only hope this little undercover operation at the library doesn't turn out to be a wild-goose chase."

Anna thought about how agitated Simone had been after looking through the vertical file yesterday morning—the way Simone had rushed out of the library without so much as a good-bye. Top that off with the fact that Anna was desperate to find her sister and nephew but was at a loss as to how to proceed, and there you had it—sneaking into the library and snooping through the files suddenly seemed like a perfectly reasonable course of action. Her jaw firmed. "Even if it does, we have to start somewhere. The vertical file is this way. Grab my keys and close the door, will you?"

Charlie did, and then followed her to a corner in the back. "What's a vertical file?"

"Sorry, that's librarian-speak. I suppose a lot of libraries don't even have vertical files anymore. But Mrs. Marlowe is—"

"A sweet old bat."

"I was going to say old school. Basically, the vertical file is just a cabinet full of newspaper clippings from the *Tangleheart Gazette*—stories that were reported before the paper went online. Mrs. Marlowe wants to be sure important articles, especially the ones about town history and locals, won't be lost to posterity. I've been meaning to scan all of the stories in for her and get rid of the clippings, but I just haven't gotten around to it yet."

"And Simone was digging through the vertical file yesterday morning?"

"With Bobby in tow. She nodded hello to me and went

straight to the back. Later, I saw her riffling through the file cabinet, and even at the time I thought it was peculiar."

"What's so peculiar about that?"

"You mean besides the fact she didn't head straight over to grill me on my love life the second she walked in? It's peculiar because even though anyone can go through the vertical file on his own, no one ever does. The vertical file is hardly ever used, and the patrons who do use it routinely ask me to find the clippings they need for them. It's certainly not Simone's style to hesitate to bother me."

Propping her hip against an oversized reading desk, she continued, "We don't allow patrons to re-file the clippings. They leave them in this basket." She indicated a large wire basket. "And then either Mrs. Marlowe or I file them back when we get time."

"Lucky for us you haven't had time." Charlie snatched the only folder in the file-back basket, and opened it, displaying its contents. "Not good."

There appeared to be at least fifty clippings in the file. While a lump rose in her throat, hope sank in her chest. Charlie was right. They were chasing wild geese, looking for needles in haystacks, wasting precious time. She busied her hands, fiddling with the buttons on her blouse.

"How are we going to figure out what Simone was looking for with all these clippings to choose from?"

Charlie cast a comforting arm around her. "You know Simone better than anyone, Anna. Something will stand out—you'll know it when you see it."

She was no psychic. The only thing she knew for certain was that her sister would never have taken Bobby away from his father over a run-of-the-mill marital spat. Simone loved Bobby, and she loved Nate. She wouldn't have run off with her infant son, knowing the worry she'd cause. Simone knew too well the way she and Anna had suffered when their own mother took off. No. Either Simone had a compelling reason for running, *or she hadn't run at all*. Her fingers stopped flying over her buttons. Her heart fluttered in her chest. A flash of tears threatened, but she blinked them back. "The police should be doing the job of trying to find Bobby and Simone, not rank amateurs like us."

Charlie used his thumb and forefinger to thump her shoulder. "Who you calling rank?"

He always knew how to make her smile, no matter the circumstance, and once again she felt grateful to have him at her side—dangerously grateful. Sliding out from under his arm, she said, "Be serious, please."

"Okay. The police think employing a conservative, watch-and-see approach is best. And I can't say for sure they're wrong about that, but I'm not really a watch-and-see kind of guy. So you tell me, Anna. Your family—your call. Do you want to start looking for Simone and Bobby on our own, or do you want to wait and let the law handle it?"

Maybe they'd find something in the news articles that would prod Hawkins into action. "I can't just sit around doing nothing." And she couldn't think straight either. "But I'm tired, and I need something to sharpen my senses. If we're going to do this, we're going to need coffee."

"Lots of it," he agreed.

"Let's go through these clippings at my place." Dropping the manila folder into her shoulder bag, she said, "I can return this file in the morning, and Mrs. Marlowe will never have to know I took it."

She snapped her bag shut.

At the same time, an explosion of sound echoed through the room, making her heart lurch.

Gunshot!

Ears ringing, she spun around.

Suddenly, Charlie was on her, throwing her to the floor, crushing her with his weight. "Stay down. Don't fucking move," he whispered urgently in her ear.

She bucked violently beneath him, gasping for air. But then he touched his cheek to hers, and she froze. *Charlie was not the enemy.* Willing herself not to let panic overtake her, she drew one shallow breath after another. A wrong move from her would put them *both* in more danger.

Clunk. Clunk. Clunk.

Heavy footfalls on hardwood.

Peering beneath the reading desk, she spotted a pair of boots about twenty feet away. Coming closer.

Closer.

These were downright predatory boots. Black leather shafts inlaid with the star of Texas. Silver alligator skin covering the toes.

She shuddered.

Charlie shifted his weight, and whispered something that sounded like *stay here* into her hair. But *here* wasn't safe, because the reading desk they were hiding behind couldn't stop a bullet. Her heart pounded against her ribs, magnifying her pulse everywhere in her body. Her ears, her wrists—even her elbows—buzzed with terror.

Crack!

Another gunshot boomed through the room. Her body recoiled, as though she'd been hit, and slivers of wood rained down from above. She reached to cover her head—found Charlie's hands protecting her—and saw a hole where the bullet had slammed through the desk, just inches from where she and Charlie lay.

Her cheek was wet.

Blood?

She swiped her hand across her skin. No, not blood.

Tears.

Charlie's lips moved against her cheek, but she couldn't decipher what he was saying at all—it sounded like a tuning fork was humming in her ear. She tried to scream but no sound came out. When she recognized the familiar sensation of her vocal cords going slack and useless, true panic—followed by an even truer determination—set in. She wasn't giving in to fear.

No fucking way.

Without notice, Charlie reared up and waved his arms.

Her throat convulsed. Past the terror, she pushed out a scream. "No!" But it was too late.

Charlie darted across the room, his words floating through the air in slow motion: "Over...here...ass...hole."

Charlie must've made it to the entrance because the lights switched off just as another shot rang out. Charlie had drawn the shooter's fire and given her the cover of darkness. He'd risked his life to give her this chance. She could not waste it.

Her brain locked into safe mode—that place where time slows down and fear enhances the ability to plan and act. Charlie had given her an opportunity, and she had damn well better take it.

Noiselessly, she eased the shoulder bag onto her back and out of her way, and then began inching across the floor on her belly. Her shirt climbed her chest, and the floor felt cold and slick against her skin. Her pupils hadn't accommodated to the darkness yet, but once they did, she knew she'd be able to see again—and so would Boots.

At the moment, though, she couldn't see more than an arm's length ahead.

Crack!

Another shot split through the cotton in her ears. She kept moving, scraping her body across the floor with one goal in mind. She might not be able to see her way, but she knew this library well. She put out her hand and patted the cold metal legs of a cabinet—the card catalogue—a familiar landmark that served to mark her route. A full-body tremor had set in, but she kept going. Around the corner, and then straight ahead.

Just another yard or so.

She needed to make it that far if she was going to get out of here.

By now her eyes had adjusted to the darkness, and with the light of the moon sifting into the room, she could see well enough to make out more than just shadows. Keeping her body flat, she lifted her head, searching the room for Charlie, praying she wouldn't find him—that he'd already made it out alive.

Please, God.

She couldn't see Charlie anywhere.

Thank you.

Then her skin went cold. Boots was there, his feet planted a few yards away, alligator toes pointed in her direction. Her gaze climbed the shiny silver vamps, up black shafts with an inlaid star of Texas. Blood surged to her face. She forced her eyes to keep going, and saw baggy jeans, dark jacket, ski mask.

Gun!

A crash sounded on the other side of the room.

Boots turned and fired a flurry of shots—too many and too fast to count.

She was breathing so hard now she thought her lungs would split wide open.

Focus.

On shaking arms, she dragged herself forward until she reached her target—the narrow section of carpet along the north side of the room. She pressed her back against the wall, and then inched up, up, up. Felt around until she found the smooth rubber handle she sought.

Yes!

Boots leapt from the shadows into a slice of moonlight, raised his arm, and pointed his pistol straight at her.

Her heart stopped. She felt the sudden absence of its beat like a blow to the chest.

Then she saw it: the open slide on the gun.

Boots was out of bullets.

He'd surely have another magazine, but she had a split second to act before he could reload.

She yanked the handle.

The fire alarm rang out, the noise reverberating through her.

Flinging her hands out in front, she found a desk and began yanking drawers, desperately searching for a weapon—a letter opener, a paperweight, *anything*. She grasped a bottle and hurled it with all her might.

It shattered against Boots's head.

A sickly sweet smell exploded in the air.

Mrs. Marlowe's brandy!

The blare of the fire alarm deafened. Boots heaved his back into a file cabinet, setting off a domino effect. She dove to the side to avoid being crushed, slamming her cheek against the hardwood floor. A breath, so big her lungs deserved a medal for having held it, rushed out.

Boots, the deadly swamp predator, was running for the door like a spooked rabbit.

6

Tangleheart: Tuesday, 12:45 A.M.

No one had followed them from the library—Charlie had made certain of it. Having put a good ten minutes between them and the scene of the crime, he guided his new Camaro to the road's soft shoulder, and then released his death grip on the steering wheel, cut the engine and turned to Anna. "You okay?"

She nodded, but her body was shaking like a child with a fever. He reached in the backseat, found his warm-up jacket and draped it around her shoulders.

"Thanks. I-I don't know why I'm cold on a night like this."

"Most likely you're a bit shocky." When he pulled his arms back to his sides, his muscles jittered beneath his skin—like he'd just bench-pressed twice his weight instead of lifting a windbreaker. "Me, too, I guess."

Their gazes met and held. Moonlight painted her face in broad strokes, leaving her skin luminous. Adrenaline had dilated her pupils and changed the soft blue of her eyes to midnight. His eyes dipped to her full lips. He leaned toward her. Ten minutes ago, they were fighting for their lives, but now, all he could think about was how much he wanted to kiss her.

Earlier, at his place, they'd nuzzled and played, and almost kissed, but Nate had interrupted them. In that moment, Charlie had been operating primarily from lust, and he had to admit that lust was still there—only now it was the least of what was driving him. He needed to feel the warmth of her body, needed to hold her in his arms for very different reasons. He needed to verify that Anna was still here, still breathing, still *alive*. He'd finally found her again after all this time, and he'd be damned if he'd lose her again.

"Anna, I..." He swallowed dryly.

"Yes?" She laid her palm on his knee and then hurriedly pulled it away.

"I...wanted to tell you...I was proud of you back there. You saved our lives."

Her mouth opened but clamped shut when headlights flashed on the road behind them. As one, they ducked. Wordlessly, they stayed down until they heard the approaching car move safely past. He sat up first and started the engine, but kept the car in park and the headlights off. They needed time to recover, time to think, but they couldn't sit here on the side of the road all night. That passing car was all the warning he needed to get the hell out of Tangleheart. "We should make some decisions," he said carefully. Anna had called nine-one-one, and then Nate, as they'd sped away from the library. The operator had given them explicit instructions, but... "I don't think we should drive to the police station."

"Agreed."

He arched an eyebrow in disbelief. "You're not going to put up an argument? Anna Kincaid is going to defy authority—just like that?"

She gave him the one-eyebrow lift right back. "I realize that while I was on my cell, you were concentrating on driving like hell, but I promise you, I told both the nine-one-one operator and Nate everything that happened—absolutely everything we know. Nate should have no problem lighting a fire under Hawkins after this. But if we go to the station, they'll confiscate this file as evidence." She lifted her purse. "The police won't have any idea which of those clippings would have meaning for Simone, but I might be able to figure something out."

Anna scanned the area surrounding the car. "Besides, the shooter obviously followed us from Nate's place to the library. Now that we've lost him, I sure don't see us marching into the station and filing a complaint. Boots is expecting us to drive straight to the authorities, and that will give him a perfect opportunity to get back on our tail. He's probably staking it out right now, waiting for us."

"*Boots*—that's what we're calling him?" *Motherfucker* seemed like a better fit to Charlie, but he supposed he could go along with whatever shorthand Anna preferred. "Okay by me. So if we're not going to the station, where are we going?" No safe place immediately sprang to mind.

"How about my father's old hunting cabin? It's about an hour's drive—isolated. And there's always a chance that's where Simone took Bobby. I should've thought of it before, although I doubt she'd go there. She always hated that place."

He pressed his fingers to his eyelids. "I'm not sure that's such a good idea. If Boots knows anything about your family, he may know about the cabin."

"Four years ago, my father wrapped his car around a tree…" Looking at him like she was unsure how much she wanted to tell him, she hesitated.

But he already knew the story. "Nate told me," he said. A few years back, Anna's father tied one on and plowed into a tree. "I heard your dad lost the use of his legs." His hand found her knee. "I'm so sorry, Anna."

"Thanks." She kept her tone matter-of-fact. "It wasn't

entirely a bad thing. He didn't die or kill anyone else, and he hasn't had a drink since. The way I look at it, that accident probably saved his life. But since then, Daddy's been unable to work. So Nate stepped in and paid off the home mortgage, but we all agreed it was best to let the hunting cabin go back to the bank. Our family hasn't owned it for years."

"But if you don't own the cabin anymore—"

"Then no one will expect us to hide there. The couple who bought it from the bank planned to tear it down and build a luxury vacation house on the property. But they must've fallen on hard times or something because they've never done a thing with the land. I think we'd be safe there. At least long enough to get our ducks in a row."

He hated to burst Anna's bubble, but one row of ducks wasn't going to stop a cold-blooded killer. Without cutting the engine, he opened his door, flicking off the overhead light just as it flashed on. "I'll be right back. I've got an HK 45 and ammo in the trunk."

7

Near Tangleheart: Tuesday, 2:00 A.M.

Anna triple-checked the front door of the cabin, making sure she'd engaged the deadbolt. Luckily, the new property owners never bothered to reset the combination on the electronic lock. The cabin and its contents were of no interest to them—they only cared about the land—and that had saved Anna and Charlie the trouble of breaking a window.

Not counting the thick layers of dust, everything inside seemed just as her family had left it, though she couldn't be certain until morning. Without electricity, they'd had to search the cabin using the flashlight feature on their cells, and now their batteries were so low they couldn't afford to use the phones as reading lights. The clippings would have to wait a few more hours—until the sun came up. The part of her brain that operated on logic told her she'd have more luck with the clippings after a few hours' rest, but her breath released in a frustrated rush anyway.

"No sign of them." She hadn't really expected to find Simone and Bobby at the cabin, but she had *hoped*. The knots in her gut told her she'd been hoping much harder than she'd realized.

At the window, Charlie let the curtains fall back. "Far as I can tell, no one's creeping around out there. I'm sure we weren't followed, so unless Boots knew where we were headed—which is impossible since we didn't know ourselves until an hour ago—we should be safe here tonight." He crossed the room to stand beside her. "I know you're disappointed Simone and Bobby aren't here, but Anna, you knew it was a long shot. I'm sure Hawkins has called in outside help by now, so at least we're not the only ones looking for them."

"We'll find them soon," she said, more to herself than to Charlie.

We have to.

"Stay positive."

"I'll try." And then she did. Closing her eyes, she imagined a fire crackling in the hearth, the smell of cedar filling the room. She licked her lips, practically tasting the hot chocolate on her tongue. This cabin was one of the few places she'd been happy as a child. Her father came up most every weekend during hunting season, plus a fair amount in summer. With no wife at home, he'd been forced to bring his girls along. Simone used to dread the isolation of the cabin, but Anna relished the chance to escape the taunts of the neighborhood bullies.

Freak! Freak! Why don't you speak?

Sometimes the most hurtful words came from the adults.

Leave her alone, kids. The poor girl's retarded.

If Simone was with her, she'd yell and curse and threaten Anna's tormentors with her fists. But Anna would simply stand there, arms locked at her sides, her knuckles aching to rise up and punch somebody smack in the face. Only she never did. She didn't fight back because good little girls didn't curse and run wild in the street. And she *needed* to be good—good enough to make her mother want to come back home.

Only, Mom never did.

And finally, Anna stopped hoping. That's when she stopped whispering, too. After all, she had Simone. And Simone had mothered her enough to drive any child stark raving mad. A small smile lifted her lips. It almost felt good, in a completely devastating sort of way, to know that the tables had turned and now Simone needed her.

At last it was her turn to look out for the sister who had always looked out for her.

Anna placed her hand over her belly and exhaled, willing herself to relax. Her limbs were wired with restless energy. She needed to go for a run to burn this tension. She needed to run and run and keep on running until every muscle in her body released its pain.

Rolling her neck to work out the kinks, she felt a strong hand come over her shoulder. A thumb started to stroke along the side of her neck, making her stomach loop and dive. When she opened her eyes, she got caught up in Charlie's gaze, marveling at the way the cool blue of his eyes had gone all smoky. She didn't know how long she'd been standing here daydreaming, or how long he'd been watching.

His knees bent, and before she could protest, he'd swooped an arm under her bottom and lifted her off the floor. "I'm sorry, Anna, but I need you *now*. I can't wait any more." His words came out in a low growl that sent shivers racing through her.

As he carried her into the bedroom, she let her head nestle against his chest, cherishing the feel of his cotton T-shirt, damp with sweat, beneath her cheek, cherishing *life*. She pressed her lips against the unyielding wall of his chest. It seemed she didn't want to protest after all.

Inside the bedroom, still holding her in his arms, Charlie managed to yank open the curtains, causing a glaze of moonlight to coat the room.

"Anna." He whispered her name, and the fine hairs on her

arms rose. On the outside her skin prickled with chill bumps, but inside she blazed, like a carefully constructed pile of kindling that had finally found its match.

"Anna." This time he moaned her name, mesmerizing her. Her limbs went slack, and she felt helpless to move. Didn't *want* to move and break the spell. Because right here and right now, there was no one else in the world. There was only Charlie, saying her name—rubbing his lips into the hollow of her throat, reminding every cell in her body that she was *alive,* and that she needed him too.

He lowered her onto the bed. The mattress creaked when he added his weight to hers, removed his shoes and socks. As she drank in the scent of him—sweat and adrenaline and male musk—prickles of excitement spread down her belly and twitched between her legs. Hurriedly, she kicked off her sandals.

On the nightstand beside the bed, a pistol flickered in the moonlight. Charlie had seen to everything, and right now all she wanted to do was lose herself in the moment. Right now all she wanted to think about was how good it felt to be with him.

Reaching out, he took her hands in his. "You're shaking."

"It's been a wild night," she replied, even though she knew that wasn't the reason she trembled. He rolled on his side, facing her. Watching her from beneath hooded lids, he worked his knee between her legs, dragging it up and down until the friction from his body and the tug of her jeans had her aching and wet. Her hand went to her mouth to muffle a soft cry.

He pulled that hand down, cupped her palm over his rockhard length. "This is what you do to me," he said, his voice low and throaty.

She fumbled with the buttons on his Levi's, and he helped her push them down.

"Talk to me, Anna. Tell me what you need."

She dipped her hand inside his boxers, cradled his erection, delighting in the slick, hot feel of him.

"Talk to me, Peaches."

Her heart fluttered nervously in her chest. Talking had never been her thing—and certainly not in bed. But she did know what she wanted. She wanted *Charlie.* She wanted him like she'd never wanted any other man.

"Naked. I want you naked." Just saying those words felt freeing and conjured up all sorts of ideas of what she wanted to do to him—what she wanted him to do to her.

"That's no problem." He wriggled on the bed, twisting out of his Levi's and boxers, while she worked his T-shirt over his head. "Now you." It wasn't a request.

She scooted out of her jeans, out of her damp panties, and then sat back on her heels. Charlie lay on his side, never taking his eyes off her as she shed her blouse, her bra—all of her protective layers. Reaching up, he caught one breast in his hand. Gently, he squeezed and played and fondled. He teased the sensitive skin around her nipple over and over again, frustrating her, driving her mad.

His eyes met hers. "Tell me, Anna."

Her heart still fluttered in her chest, but she was no longer nervous. She didn't know what it was about Charlie that made her so bold, but it didn't matter. She liked feeling this way.

She'd never been in so much danger, and yet she'd never felt so safe.

She moved his fingers to her hardened nipples. "I want to feel your mouth on me, here."

"Not right now."

She started to complain, but by then he'd pushed her legs wide, and she changed her mind about where she wanted to feel his mouth.

"You're so beautiful," he said, slipping his thumb between

her folds, and working it in slow circles over her until she wanted to scream. At last, he put his mouth on her.

She writhed against him, wanting more, so much more.

"Please." She gasped and tugged him up by the shoulders until he lay on top of her.

He snuck his arms around her and rolled on his back, leaving her on top, straddling his hips. She took a moment to let her eyes feast on his body—the honed, hard muscles of his chest and arms, his flat, tanned stomach. She started to move down, wanting to taste him, wanting to drive him to the brink, as he'd done to her, but he clasped her wrists and dragged her back up. "Next time."

Her hands gripped the sheets on the bed. He'd spoken as if he were certain there would be a next time. She couldn't think about that now. She couldn't think at all.

Charlie spread her open and positioned her how he wanted her, with the head of his erection pressing against her opening.

"Kiss me," he said.

His words rippled through her like tiny shock waves.

Impossible.

They'd shared so much, been through so much together, and yet they'd never shared a kiss—not a real one. His lips had been on her hands, her neck, her back—her most intimate places—but they'd never…

"Yes," she said. "I will."

Her heart hammered in her chest. *This* was what she longed for. More than anything. She bent her face to his, and he dropped his head back in surrender. She relished taking the lead, brushing her lips over his, curling her fingers through his thick, sweat-dampened hair. His mouth opened beneath hers, and their tongues met and tangled, slowly at first, and then urgently.

His hands found her hips and guided her back in place.

Slowly, she let him stretch her, enter her, fill her. She rubbed her breasts and belly over him, and he moved inside her, following her rhythm, letting her set the pace. The pleasure built and built. She wanted to prolong the sensation, but her control was too thin. With her next small movement, his next upward thrust, her muscles clenched around him. One climax ended, and then a second wave engulfed her. He bucked beneath her and let out a loud, guttural moan. Pressure welled inside her yet again, but it wasn't only her orgasm—this was something more, something coming from deep, deep inside. While her body trembled around him, her throat convulsed from the effort of containing her cries.

"Let it go, sweetheart. It's safe here." His hand found hers.

She looked at Charlie's beautiful face, and then a series of loud, primal moans came shuddering out of her mouth. Joy poured through her, lifting her heart. She was making *noise*—a lot of it, and it felt so damn good.

8

Near Tangleheart: Tuesday, 6:00 A.M.

CHARLIE GLANCED IN the cabin's bathroom mirror, dragged his fingers through his bed-head and slammed a hard brake on the emotions that made it hard to swallow, hard to breathe. When they'd awakened this morning, Anna turned away from his kiss—and it hurt like hell. But now was not the time to challenge her.

They'd taken a few hours to rest, just until the first light of morning began sifting through the cabin windows—it would've been futile to work by moonlight, and they needed sleep badly. Grateful the property owners had kept the water on, if not the electricity, he washed his hands, and then exited the bathroom.

He found Anna already in the kitchen. The sun's first rays pinked her skin and floated a halo of light above her freshly brushed hair. Her bloodshot eyes sported dark circles below. She looked like an angel—one who'd just pulled a double shift at Billy Bob's.

A square of old poster board had been laid out on the picnic-style table, and some colored pens leaned in a jelly-jar glass. Apparently, librarians carried colored pens in their purses.

Anna had removed the newspaper clippings from the folder and judging from her assorted piles, she'd wasted no time getting started on them.

"Morning, beautiful." He slipped an arm around her waist and kissed the back of her neck.

He couldn't help himself.

Her shoulders jumped, and she quickly slipped out of his embrace. Clearing her throat, she pointed to the warped poster board on the tabletop. "I thought we'd make a murder board."

Uncomprehending, and more than a little put off, he turned his palms up.

"You know, like the one Beckett uses on *Castle*. I think it's a good way to get organized, and I want to—"

"Get our ducks in a row." He didn't have a clue what Beckett did on *Castle,* but he was in for a penny already. "So we're going to stop a killer and find Simone and Bobby by using petrified poster board, colored pens and...your knowledge of television crime shows? Have I got that right?"

Worry welled in her eyes. Instantly, he regretted his sarcasm. Beneath her cheerful facade, Anna was terrified, and with good reason. Her sister was missing. Mere hours ago, a gunman had ambushed them. And now, while Anna was keeping a stiff upper lip and trying to make the best of dire circumstances, he was busy acting like a jackass because she didn't kiss him good morning. It was time for him to get his head on straight and be the man she needed him to be.

"Hang on a minute." He hurried to the bedroom and back, and then laid his pistol on the table next to the murder board. "You know anything about guns?"

"A little. Daddy used to keep them. He took me target shooting a few times."

"Tell you what, then. You show me how to work a murder

board, and I'll refresh your memory on how to work a firearm. Okay?"

"Okay." She used the back of her hand to wipe a dab of moisture from her cheek, and sent him a hopeful smile.

And all he'd had to do to cheer her up was stop being a dick.

That wasn't so hard.

After removing the magazine and making sure there was no bullet in the chamber, he handed her his empty gun. "This is a semiautomatic pistol, an HK 45. It's the compact model, so you should be able to handle it. Ten bullets in the magazine."

She held out her hand.

"Careful."

With the gun pointed safely away, she snapped the magazine in place.

"That's good," he said, impressed by the no-nonsense way she handled the weapon.

Beaming under his approval, she said, "I remembered how to load a pistol."

"Here." He put his hands over hers and showed her what to do next. "Now you're cocked and locked. All you have to do is flip the safety off and you're ready to roll."

She set the gun back on the table and pulled a red pen from the jelly jar. "My turn. Let's make a murder board—starting with a timeline. We'll add anything that comes to mind, whether we think it's important or not." Then she wrote: *Sunday afternoon—Simone and Bobby go missing.*

That didn't seem quite right. "I think we should start the timeline earlier. After all, something important must've happened beforehand, leading up to Simone's disappearance," he said.

"You're right. There had to have been an inciting incident. Let's go back at least to your welcome home dinner on Saturday night. We can backtrack further if we think of something."

Glancing up, Anna caught him staring. "Why are you looking at me that way?"

"I was just thinking how pretty you look when you worry your bottom lip between your teeth like that."

Sweet Jesus, Charlie. Never say anything like that out loud again.

Her face lifted in a full-on smile.

Maybe just once more...

But it was too late.

She was all business again. "What do you remember happening at the dinner party?"

Wanting to keep the mood light as well as do justice to his own role in this simulated Castle-Beckett crime-fighting exercise, he conjured an answer by rubbing his forehead. "Nate and Simone were happy as clams. He gave her an emerald necklace, and then that picture of Catherine Timmons came on the news."

He leaned his elbows on the table. *This murder board thing might actually work.* "Write that down. Catherine Timmons was found dead. Gunshot wound to the head...just like Megan."

Anna got it all down, and then her hand flew to her mouth. "I completely forgot about the letter." She added the word LETTER in all caps. "I didn't think much of it at the time, but Simone was flustered because she found a letter addressed to Nate in a woman's handwriting."

"What woman?"

Anna shook her head. "I don't know. I practically ordered Simone not to open the envelope. I told her to give it to Nate." She looked up, wide-eyed. "I wish to God I'd opened that letter with her."

As much as he understood Anna's regret, he didn't indulge it. He'd learned the hard way not to dwell on past mistakes. If you did, it might cost you today's chance.

He picked up a pen of his own, a green one, and started making notes on the board, scribbling and thinking aloud.

"Sunday morning, Simone went to the library and later withdrew money from the bank." His chin started to itch. "After the bank, Simone took Bobby to her in-laws' house. No one has seen them since."

He scratched the whiskers that had sprouted overnight, and then wrote: *Simone lied*.

"Yes. She lied about changing Bobby's diaper."

He hadn't expected Anna to react that way. Instead of rushing to Simone's defense, she'd considered the facts objectively.

"Simone forgot to change Bobby's diaper. Or maybe she didn't plan to change his diaper at all," she added.

Simone, by all accounts, was hypersensitive to her baby's needs. "I don't get it."

Anna tilted her head. "Me either. So that means it must be important—because it's so out of character."

He tended to agree, although he had no idea how Simone's strange visit to Lila and Caleb Carlisle's home fit into the puzzle. He fell silent and began pacing the kitchen.

While he paced, Anna turned back to the newspaper clippings, flipping them facedown as she finished each story. Soon, the light in the kitchen grew bright. So bright that something he hadn't seen before, not last night, not earlier this morning, caught his eye. "Anna..."

Intent on studying her stories, she didn't answer.

This cabin had supposedly been empty for years. He tried again. "Anna, did you put a piece of paper in the trash can?"

She waved him off. "I haven't got any paper—not except the clippings, I mean."

Someone else—*Simone* maybe—had been here before them. He grabbed the wadded-up paper from the trash and went to Anna's side.

At the table, Anna skimmed her finger over yet another

headline, and suddenly the color drained from her face. "I think this is it!"

Her hand trembled as she spread the newspaper article in the center of the murder board.

Remembering Megan O'Neal.

It wasn't so much the title as the *author* that caused Charlie to take a stunned step backward.

By Nathan Carlisle.

Charlie's temples throbbed unpleasantly. A dull ache spread across his forehead. And no matter how hard he blinked, the name on the byline stared menacingly back at him, unchanged.

Nathan Carlisle.

Charlie pounded a fist on his thigh. A disturbing idea was worming its way into his head. "Nate wrote a tribute piece to Megan."

"The story was so heartfelt, I remember, at the time, thinking Nate should try his hand at journalism." Anna looked up, troubled. "Of course, he never did."

Charlie's hands clenched into fists. In his mind, he could hear the puzzle pieces clicking ominously into place. It wasn't easy to keep his voice steady, but for Anna's sake he tried. "It must've been *Nate*. Nate was the man Megan was seeing while I was away."

He dreaded opening the paper he'd pulled from the trash. But there was no use putting it off. On a deep inhale, he said, "I think Simone has been here." He spread the paper open on the table. "This looks like expensive stationery. It could be the letter that Simone intercepted on Saturday night."

Anna's eyes lit up. They were onto something. She began reading the short letter aloud. At first, her voice was soft, but it grew stronger and more determined with every word:

I know what you did to Megan. The necklace is the key.

The letter was signed: *C.T.*

They scanned the murder board and said in unison, "Catherine Timmons!"

"But what does it mean, *the necklace is the key*?" Anna closed her eyes, concentrating. "Is this about the necklace Nate gave Simone on Saturday night?"

"No." Charlie knew exactly which necklace was *the key*. He wished like hell he didn't, but he did. Pointing his finger to the picture of Megan—the one in the newspaper article—he said, "Look."

In the photo, Megan wore the necklace Charlie had made for her in shop class, all those years ago—an antique-style key on a silver chain. "This is the necklace Catherine Timmons meant. This is *the key*."

He refrained from adding that he'd told Megan it was the key to his heart. That had been a lie.

It had always been Anna who held that key.

"Mrs. O'Neal told me Megan wore that necklace every day. But after she died, it was never recovered," he explained.

Anna dropped into a chair. Her lips had gone white. "*I know what you did to Megan.*"

He dumped the pens out of the jelly-jar glass, went to the sink and filled the jar with water. "Megan didn't kill herself—she was murdered, and Catherine Timmons figured it out. Then Catherine Timmons was murdered—because she knew too much." He handed Anna the glass of water.

"*If* that's really the letter Simone found, it came in an envelope addressed to Nate. That suggests *Nate* killed Megan...and the reporter." Anna gulped the water. "Only, Nate never got the letter, so how would he know Catherine was on to him? Why would he go after her?"

"He could've found out any number of ways, if Timmons had been nosing around for months. Simone must've taken Bobby and run because she—"

"No. Simone would never believe Nate murdered those women." Anna's voice sounded plaintive. "Do you?"

"I don't *want* to believe Nate is capable of murder, no. But I have to admit that I'm glad we didn't tell him where we were headed."

Anna held her head up stoically. "Let's review the facts…or what we suppose to be the facts. Catherine Timmons sent a letter to Nate implying that she knew he murdered Megan. Catherine is found dead, and for the sake of this exercise, let's assume that even though Nate never saw the letter, somehow he knew she was on to him—and murdered her to keep her quiet."

Anna's determined calm amazed him. "Okay. That's reasonable, given the information we have on hand."

"Of course, we're assuming Simone didn't take my advice. She read the letter in private, and it frightened her."

Charlie picked up the thread. "Simone suspected Nate murdered Megan and Catherine Timmons. But like us, she didn't want to believe it. She remembered the article Nate wrote about Megan. She went to the library looking for it, hoping to find something in it to dispel her suspicions. Instead, she found a gut-wrenching article that sounded like it had been written by Megan's lover, and a photo of Megan wearing a key necklace."

Anna held up her hand. "Even assuming all that, I still don't believe Simone would be convinced. She wouldn't take Bobby and run unless she feared for her life. And she wouldn't believe Nate murdered those women…" Her voice broke. "Not unless…"

Charlie smacked the chair next to him and sent it crashing to the floor. "Simone found the necklace among Nate's things. That's why Simone took Bobby and ran. *Simone found the key.*"

Charlie grabbed his cell and bounded to his feet. "I'm going to drive up the road and try to get signal. We need to update Hawkins."

Anna shoved her chair back, but didn't get up. "If Simone

and Bobby have been here, they might still be close by. I should stay here, in case they come back."

Anna was right, and she'd be as safe here as anywhere. He lifted her onto her feet and pulled her into his arms. Her heart beat wildly against his. Not giving her a chance to refuse him, he kissed her hard on the mouth. She kissed him back with such ferocity she nearly bit him and then broke the embrace.

He hurried to the door, halting at the threshold. He didn't dare look back at her face.

"Anna..." His heart clenched as he ground out the next words. "Keep that pistol cocked and locked."

∾

ANNA STOOD IN THE DOORWAY, watching Charlie's Camaro disappear down the gravel road. Her head felt heavy and light at the same time. Other than a single glass of water this morning, she hadn't had anything to eat or drink since Jenny Jacoby had served them tea on Monday evening. Anna went to the sink and filled a cup with water, gulped it down and then did it again. If she didn't stay hydrated, she was likely to faint, and fainting was not acceptable. Not at a time like this.

With her head starting to clear, she glanced around the kitchen. Now that it was light out, she ought to search the cabin again. If Simone left the letter behind, she might have left other things too. Maybe Anna would find a map, or a receipt for airline tickets, or maybe she'd find...

Nothing.

Her heart kicked up.

Nothing was exactly what she found when her gaze landed on the hook by the kitchen window. For as long as her family had owned this cabin, a set of keys to the nearest neighbor's farmhouse had hung on that hook. Her father had a key to the neighbor's place in order to keep an eye on things when it was vacant. It was possible the farmhouse keys had been taken down by the cabin's new owners...but they didn't seem to have moved anything else.

She checked her cell.

No service.

No surprise.

How long had Charlie been gone?

She checked her watch.

Minutes.

It could be half an hour, maybe more, before he returned.

Her cheeks flushed hot. Why hadn't she noticed the missing keys right away? It seemed so obvious now. The least likely place anyone would expect Simone to hide was the one place Simone hated even more than she hated this cabin: the now-abandoned farmhouse Megan rented that horrible summer.

Six years ago, Simone went looking for fun, looking for lively company to relieve the isolation of a weekend at the cabin. Simone had gone to that farmhouse looking for Megan O'Neal, and she'd found her...lying in a pool of blood.

That was the last time Simone ever let their father drag her anywhere near these woods. No one would ever expect Simone to go to the farmhouse—it was the perfect place to hide.

Anna's nerves were jumping all over her body. Now that she thought she knew where to find Simone and Bobby, she had to go to them—and she had to go *now*. She scribbled a note for Charlie and grabbed the gun.

9

Near Tangleheart: Tuesday, 6:45 A.M.

BRANCHES CRUNCHED BENEATH Anna's shoes and a fine mist of rain dampened her face as she ran full-tilt up the road. It'd taken her mere minutes to scramble down the path from the cabin. Now she was headed up Farm Road 99 as hard and as fast as her legs would carry her. Her strides grew longer and more fluid by the minute. Her entire body hummed with energy—with purpose. Her breathing hitched along steadily. She was nowhere near winded. It was as if she'd been training for this moment her entire life. Hanging by its straps around her neck, her purse banged against her chest.

Inside the purse: Charlie's HK 45.

Cocked and locked.

Not until she sighted the old farmhouse did fear begin to drip into her veins, diluting the confidence that had been fueling her. There were plenty of places a shooter might be hiding: in that copse of chinaberry bushes to her right, for example, or maybe behind that up-ended wagon to her left. She slowed to a walk for caution's sake. Tire tracks marked the road, but she didn't see Simone's car in the drive. Most likely she would've parked farther up the road or pulled off into the trees somewhere along the way.

Anna dug out her pistol and tossed her cumbersome purse behind a bush. Taking cover wherever she could find it, she made her way to the house, up the steps and onto the front porch. There was no concealing the creak of the old planks no matter how stealthily she moved. Her breath hardened to concrete in her lungs.

Just take it nice and easy.

She tried the door.

Unlocked.

Her lungs relaxed. She sucked in a blast of oxygen, straight-armed the .45 and slipped through the door.

No sooner had she ducked inside than her ears pricked at the sound of Nate's voice in another room. *Dear God.* He'd found Simone. He knew his wife too well.

Anna heard crying, and her gut clenched.

Bobby!

She inched her finger closer to the trigger. Elbows locked, sweeping her gun in front of her as she moved, she spun across the room and reached a cracked-open door. Noiselessly, she positioned herself to peer through the slit.

Her heart climbed to her throat.

Nate was perched on a hard-back chair and, as she'd seen him do on many occasions, he was bouncing his young son on one knee.

She covered her mouth to muffle the wheeze that escaped her throat. Simone huddled against the opposite wall, in a pale, stricken heap. Anna tightened her grip on her pistol. Her arm trembled all the way from her shoulder to her wrist. She couldn't risk firing at Nate with Bobby on his knee. She wasn't that good a shot. No one was that good a shot.

Lowering her arm to her side, she tried to catch Simone's eye. But it was no use. Simone's gaze was fixed on Bobby.

Anna tensed, arched on the balls of her feet, as she watched her sister uncurl into a stand and take a dangerous step toward Nate.

"Give me the baby, and I promise not to run," Simone said.

Nate's knee bounced up and down fast and then faster. Bobby stopped whimpering and squealed with delight.

"Please, I-I'll do anything you say." Tears leaked from Simone's eyes, slipped down her paper-white cheeks. "Let's just go home. I promise I won't tell anyone what you did to Megan."

Nate bounced Bobby higher. "I know you're mad about Megan. You have a right to be. But this is crazy, Simone. You're acting like you're scared of me."

Anna pressed her face closer to the door. Simone cowered in terror, but...if Nate had a weapon, Anna couldn't see it from where she stood.

"I *am* scared of you." Simone sobbed into her hands. "You murdered Megan and that reporter too."

When Nate bolted to his feet, Anna used her thumb to click the safety off her gun. But she kept her finger off the trigger. Bobby was still in his father's arms.

"What the hell are you talking about?" Nate's face flushed beefy red. "Yes. I had an affair with Megan while you and I were dating. I admit I got her pregnant. I'm a horrible coward not to have told you, and I know I'm to blame for her suicide, but for God's sake, Simone, you can't honestly believe I *murdered* her."

Simone's legs started to wobble.

Nate rushed to her side, gently let Bobby down and put out his hand to his wife. "Take it easy, honey. Let me help you."

Rather than collapse, Simone took Nate's hand long enough to lower herself to the floor. Then she jerked away and scrambled on her knees to her son. Bobby crawled eagerly into his mother's arms.

Nate crouched beside them. "You have to believe me, Simone. I love you and Bobby more than my life."

Simone rocked Bobby, her lips set in a hard line, her eyes glazed and empty. Suddenly, she pulled her shoulders up and sat ramrod straight. "Then explain this." She dug something shiny from her pocket and held it out for him to see. "I found *this* in your room—hidden in the back of a picture frame."

Megan's necklace.

Anna could see the old-fashioned key dangling from a chain.

"What is that?" Nate's brows knit in confusion. "Why would I hide a necklace...why would I hide *anything* from you in a bedroom we share?"

Hugging Bobby close, Simone climbed to her feet and faced her husband with a deadly calm. "Very good, Nate. You've got the act down pat. But you know perfectly well I meant that I found this in your old bedroom *at your parents' house.*" She threw the necklace down and stomped it with her heel. "The letter said *the necklace is the key.* When I didn't find it at our house, I hoped it wasn't true. I started to believe in you again. I *wanted* to believe in you so badly, because—God help me—I love you. Even now, I love you, Nate."

The way Simone's chin shivered made Anna's entire body tremble with fury at what Nate had done, not only to Megan and that reporter, but to her beloved sister.

"But then, I found the necklace in your old bedroom." Simone's voice shattered into a thousand pieces. "Right alongside your football trophies."

Reality hit Anna so hard she gagged. Lowering her head and her gun at the same time, she fended off her queasiness, somehow managed not to vomit. *So it was all true.* Her sister's husband, a man Anna had known and trusted most of her life, was the same cold-blooded monster who'd murdered two innocent women and ambushed her in the library.

From her hiding place in the hallway, Anna couldn't fire her pistol with any chance of success. Nor could she push open the door and enter the room without alerting Nate to her presence.

He could very well have a gun tucked into his jeans, and he was standing so close to Simone he was practically on top of her.

Her heart slammed against her ribs. She was going in—she had to. She wouldn't shoot unless Nate forced her hand, but she had to get Simone and Bobby out of that room. As she raised her gun, she felt hot breath on the back of her neck. A scream rose in her throat, but her vocal cords froze—no sound came out.

She started to turn, but a powerful hand gripped her wrist.

Twisted.

She heard a bone snap—and then felt a sickening pain shoot up her arm.

Her pistol dropped and slid across the floor far enough that she lost sight of it.

A swift kick swept her feet out from under her.

As she crashed to the floor, she jerked her arms up to protect her head.

Next came three rapid kicks to the back. The pain that shot up her spine cost her dearly—coating her senses with black, inky poison. For a moment, she couldn't move.

Get up!

She struggled to her knees, hands balled into fists. But she could see nothing in front of her, only darkness. She was going to pass out.

No!

Fighting to stay conscious, she blinked furiously, and at once her vision returned. She was too pissed off to give up.

A foot kicked her again from the front, and this time,

through the thick haze that varnished her senses, she recognized them:

Black leather shafts, inlaid star of Texas, silver alligator toes.

Boots kicked her in the gut, over and over again. When he bent, she smelled his foul, tobacco-stained breath. An oily, bloated face floated in front of her. "I knew you Kincaid girls would have each other's backs." Then Caleb Carlisle stuck the cold barrel of a pistol against her head and dragged her to her feet.

~

ANNA'S TEMPLES THROBBED, her eyeballs vibrated, and her head ached like a migraine on steroids. Even her runner's legs had finally given up—her thighs shook from the simple task of bearing her weight. At this point, the only thing she could do to keep herself upright was to press her hips and back against the west wall of the room—which was exactly what Caleb Carlisle, aka Boots, had instructed her to do. Simone huddled at Anna's side, clasping Bobby close. By some miracle, Bobby had fallen asleep, and now nuzzled his face contentedly against Simone's chest.

Morning light lasered through the sliding glass doors on the east side of the room, nearly blinding Anna. When she tried to raise her right hand to block the sun from her eyes, exquisite pain stopped her. She gritted her teeth and used her left hand instead.

As for Nate, he stood with his feet spread wide, arms splayed, shielding his wife and son with his body. A little more than arm's length away, Caleb wagged his gun, despite the fact that his own son and grandson were in the line of fire.

Rubbing his pistol against his cheek, Caleb scowled. "Step away from the ladies, Nathan, and take my grandson with you."

Simone tried to press Bobby into Nate's arms, but Nate shook his head. His throat worked in a long swallow, and he took a shuddering breath. "Put down the gun, Dad. I'm asking you, I'm *begging* you, to just put down the gun before somebody gets hurt."

Either Nate was completely confused about what was happening, or he was some actor.

"It's a little late for that, son. Somebody already got hurt. Now take Bobby and do like I say or I can't be responsible for what happens."

"Do whatever you want with me, but let them go...please, Dad...sir."

Caleb raised an elbow to wipe the sweat away from his hairline, and then shifted forward on his feet into a more predatory stance, if that was possible. "Get out of my way, boy, or else—"

Nate's body canted forward, and then in a blur of motion, he lunged at Caleb, grabbed his arm, and kneed him in the groin. Caleb let out a yelp, and pandemonium broke loose. Simone was screaming, Bobby was crying, and somewhere amid the noise, Anna heard a gun clatter to the floor. Her eyes widened as Caleb's pistol spun toward her like a hockey puck. Watching the gun spin intensified her wooziness—she felt like a child trapped on Mr. Toad's Wild Ride.

Caleb threw an uppercut to Nate's jaw. Nate's head snapped back. Simone screamed louder. Bobby cried harder. Anna felt a painfully heavy weight in her hand. Looking down, she managed to refocus her eyes.

When had she grabbed the gun?

Her arm throbbed, and she noticed blood on her skin. Her gun hand tipped at an unnatural angle. Bringing her left hand up to support her right wrist, she stuck the pistol out in front of her. "Back away, Caleb. All the way to the wall."

His cheeks lifted in a taunting smile. Cupping his hand

behind his ear, he said, "I can't hear you. What's that you say, *freak*?"

She tightened her grip on the gun, commanding her arms not to shake, willing her face into a hard mask. "Back against the wall, Caleb."

"Hang on there, Miss Kincaid." A deep voice echoed through the room. She wanted to shout for joy when Sheriff Hawkins came trotting in with his weapon drawn and a pair of handcuffs dangling from his belt. "Somebody wanna tell me what the hell just went down here?"

"My dad—" Nate started to speak, but Hawkins put up his hand.

Eyeing Nate warily, Hawkins hitched his chin Anna's way. "I'd like to hear it from the lady, if you don't mind."

"Caleb Carlisle's the man who ambushed Charlie and me in the library. He attacked me again today, and—"

Simone stepped forward and pointed a shaky finger at Caleb. "It was *you*! You murdered Megan. And you kept her necklace for a trophy."

Hawkins's brows snapped together. "That right, Caleb? You kill that poor girl?"

Caleb stood mute, his body stiff and unmoving. His cocky expression had vanished.

Simone retrieved the necklace from where she'd thrown it to the floor. "I have proof. I found Megan's necklace in Caleb's house. I made a terrible, terrible mistake. I suspected my own husband, when the whole time it was *him*..." She shook her fist at Caleb. "He's the murderer."

Hawkins frowned. "You ran away on your own then, because you were scared? Your husband hasn't harmed you?"

"Yes. And no. God no." Simone went to Nate and laid her head on his shoulder.

Hawkins's tense expression relaxed by a fraction. "Good."

Keeping his weapon trained on Carlisle, Hawkins sidled up to Anna. "I appreciate your help, Miss Kincaid. I'm gonna wanna hear all about how you managed to apprehend this asshole as soon as we get..." His gaze flicked to her wrist and back up. "What the hell happened to your arm?"

Awareness pricked along the nerves in Anna's wrist and hand. She could suddenly feel the pain of a thousand ice-picks chipping away at her bone. Her arm threatened to collapse under the weight of the gun in her hand. "I think he—I think Caleb broke my wrist."

Hawkins reached back and held out his open palm for Anna's gun. "Careful."

Heaving a sigh of relief, Anna pointed the pistol to the floor and handed it off to the sheriff.

Then he flashed her a twisted smile that sent a chill racing down her spine.

"Is backup on the way?" she asked. "Did Charlie explain..." Her voice trailed off. As Hawkins stalked across the room, she saw a gun that looked like *her* gun shoved in the back of his pants.

"Charlie? You mean Drex? Drex didn't explain a damn thing." A smug, satisfied look slithered over Hawkins's face. "It was my buddy Caleb, here, who brung me to the party."

Rage raced through her body like a forest fire, burning straight through her fear, burning straight through her pain. *So. That's how Hawkins had gotten here so fast—he must've been right outside the whole time.*

Hawkins handed Caleb the gun she'd just surrendered. "This is one helluva mess you got us in now, boss."

Hawkins was smiling, but Anna could see a tic setting in around his eyes. The man was nervous, scared.

Nate had blocked Simone and Bobby with his body again.

Anna read disbelief on Nate's face, and disbelief was dangerous. Denial could make you do foolish things.

Nate confronted his father. "We can get past this. Just tell me why. Why did you kill Megan?"

"It doesn't matter, son. Now, take little Bobby over there and stay the hell out of our way." Caleb jerked his chin to the east wall—the one with the sliding glass door.

Nate shook his head. "I'm your son, for God's sake. I deserve an answer."

Caleb looked at Bobby and then back at Nate. "I'll explain once, but after this, don't ever bring up that whore, Megan, to me again."

Hawkins's knee jittered, and he pulled one hand over his face. "What the hell, Caleb? You said no witnesses."

No witnesses!

Anna inched closer to her sister and mouthed the words, *Run on my go.* Simone hesitated, looked down at Bobby in her arms, and then shifted her chin in what Anna interpreted as a nod.

"*No witnesses* means no witnesses, Caleb. Bobby is one thing, but we can't let Nate go anymore than we can let the girls go," Hawkins's voice cajoled, as he purred out the words like a nervous cat.

Ignoring the sheriff, Carlisle kept his attention on Nate. "Megan was no good. I know you liked her, but to her you were nothing but a golden ticket. And when you knocked her up, she thought that baby of yours was going to get her a free ride for life on the Carlisle gravy train...sort of like the one you've had. When she lost the kid, she didn't want to give up her golden ticket. She tried to extort money from me, son. She was going to cry rape."

"But I never forced her. She had nothing on me." Nate took a step forward and met his father's eyes.

"I didn't know if you'd forced her or not. And frankly, son, I didn't care. I didn't want *my* good name dragged through the mud. Besides, I offered to pay her." He shrugged. "Not to keep quiet, though. I offered her fifty dollars to suck my dick, and the little bitch laughed in my face. Said she wouldn't blow me if her life depended on it." A low chuckle punctuated his words. "So I shot her in the head. With a remark like that, she practically dared me."

Hawkins, who'd been pacing the room during his partner's speech, pulled up short at Caleb's side. "We *can't* let him go."

Carlisle waved his pistol impatiently. "Don't piss yourself, Sheriff. I can control my boy, just like I control everyone else. You'll see."

∼

CHARLIE CROUCHED INSIDE the entryway of the old farmhouse, peering into the side room through the cracked-open door. *So this was why Hawkins hadn't picked up any of his calls; he was too busy covering Caleb Carlisle's tracks.* He could feel a scalding heat blister across his chest and prickle down his arms. Those sons of bitches made his skin crawl.

He flexed his right hand, willing a gun to appear. But that wasn't going to happen. He'd left his pistol with Anna, and now it looked to be stuffed down the back of Hawkins's pants. Charlie did a count.

First guns, and then innocents:

Hawkins: one gun in the hand, one in the pants, possible backup heat.

Carlisle: one gun in the hand, possible backup heat.

Civilian count: two women, a baby, and one screwed-up best friend.

Only an asshole would go charging into a scenario like this

one. Somebody would wind up dead, and in his experience, motherfuckers were always the last ones to die. Ideas sifted through his mind, sorting themselves into *no ways* and *maybes*. He didn't have a weapon, but at least he had his wits.

He'd rather have his gun, but sometimes you gotta make do.

First order of business was to improve the odds, and that meant he had to get one sonofabitch to come to him, leaving the other behind in the room. As hard as it was to walk away, he simply had no choice.

As quietly as possible, he made his way back outside—and then he went exploring. By the looks of the place, no one had lived here in years, so no potted plants to smash. If he remembered correctly, there was a sliding glass door on the east side of the house. That would get him into the room, all right, but not before Caleb and Hawkins could spot him, and he needed the advantage of a surprise attack.

If he could just lure one of the men to the back of the house, he could subdue him, confiscate his pistol, and then sneak back in through the front.

But how to set the trap?

There had to be something around this godforsaken place he could use. A glint of reflected sunlight caught his attention. He ducked his head around the corner to check it out and sure enough, there it was: his made-to-order distraction.

Old tin trash cans.

No time to waste debating the wisdom of his plan. It was the only one he had. He lifted a lid in each hand and banged them together, again and again. Imagining the trash can lids as Caleb and Hawkins's heads, he made one hell of a ruckus.

∼

ANNA DIDN'T KNOW how long Hawkins and Caleb had been bickering, but the longer the men argued, the more time she had to come up with a plan. Her thoughts were racing when, from somewhere outside, a loud, tinny, cacophony interrupted, repeated, and crescendoed.

Anna's heart leapt.

Charlie!

That had to be Charlie.

"What the hell?" Hawkins jumped and spun toward the sound.

Maybe he might piss himself after all.

"Sounds like...trash cans. Probably a raccoon, but you better check it out," Caleb said.

"Me?" Hawkins peered around the room like a schoolgirl who'd just seen a mouse and needed a chair to climb.

"How the hell did a little chickenshit like you ever make sheriff?" Caleb snickered. "Oh yeah. I pulled the strings that got you where you are today. So stop with the bullshit and go check out that noise."

Hawkins's expression hardened. "Whatever you say, boss." He started toward the door and then turned. "Just one thing I gotta take care of first." He raised his arm.

A booming noise.

A muzzle flash.

Scarlet bloomed onto the front of Nate's shirt.

Anna's muscles went taut and she heard Simone scream.

Nate fell back onto Simone, and together, they crumpled to the ground. Covered in crimson spatters, Simone hovered on hands and knees beside Nate, sobbing. Wailing, Bobby crawled through a pool of his father's blood.

As he turned to face his partner, Hawkins's whole body suddenly shrank. Sweat beaded his brow, dripping from his nose onto his upper lip. "I had to do it, Caleb. You would've let him run the minute I was out this door."

Caleb's arm lifted slowly, deliberately.

∼

Charlie was starting to feel a little smug, a little smarter than he ought to, banging on those trash cans when suddenly...

Crack!

The unmistakable sound of gunfire.

No more time for wits and strategy.

He ran like hell to the nearest entry point, the glass door on the east wall of the house, just in time to see Caleb Carlisle raise his arm and point his gun at Hawkins.

A loud boom followed a muzzle flash.

Hawkins's chest jerked, and his body blew back against the wall.

Nate lay in a pool of blood—one arm twitching.

Charlie grabbed a patio chair, smashed it through the sliding glass door. Then he followed the chair, diving into the room in a hailstorm of glass and thunder.

Inside the room, his assessment was lightning fast.

Two men down.

Caleb—still armed.

Charlie sprang over Nate's body and tackled Carlisle from behind. The SOB bent at the waist, and Charlie took an elbow in the gut. An *elbow* couldn't stop Charlie. He climbed Caleb like a bronco, locked onto his gun hand and twisted with all his might. When that didn't work, he used his thumb to put pressure on the radial nerve, the underside of Carlisle's wrist, and Carlisle's grip slackened, sending the gun clattering to the floor.

Carlisle growled and bucked harder.

Charlie rode the adrenaline-fueled bull, doing his damnedest to steer Caleb away from the women. Charlie's arms burned from the tight chokehold he had on Carlisle, but he wouldn't let go. He'd ride this motherfucker all night long if he had to.

"Run! Run!" Anna screamed at her sister.

Simone grabbed Bobby and fled out the front.

Enraged, Carlisle reared up with a vengeance.

Charlie kicked him hard in the sides. Carlisle reared again, and this time Charlie lost hold and went flying through the air. With a loud crack, he landed on his back. Before he could scramble to his feet, Carlisle grabbed his pistol again and aimed it straight at him. The barrel of that gun was the deepest, darkest hole Charlie had ever looked down.

His breath stormed out of his body. The beats of his heart sounded like they were coming out of stereo speakers. Then time gave him one last gift: it slowed down long enough for his gaze to dart around and find his Anna.

Sweet Jesus.

Anna had a gun—in a two-handed grip, pointed at Carlisle from across the room.

"Drop it!" She stepped forward.

Charlie's heart did a somersault in his chest.

Be careful, he mouthed.

Carlisle didn't turn. He kept his gun trained on Charlie and ground out, "You're not going to shoot me, Anna, you scared little *freak*. So why don't *you* drop it, and we can work something out?"

"Drop it! Or I'll blow your *motherfucking* head off!" Anna yelled at the top of her lungs.

Carlisle wheeled on Anna. His pistol arrowed her way.

Charlie catapulted to his feet, just as Anna's arms jerked.

He heard a deafening boom.

Carlisle staggered forward a few steps, and then hit the floor, a gun in his hand and a gaping hole in his head—just like Megan O'Neal.

10

THREE WEEKS LATER

Tangleheart: Saturday, 7:30 P.M.

Before Charlie had a chance to knock, Simone threw open the front door and motioned him inside the entryway to her home.

"I won't be out late, I promise. If you need anything at all, just call. I can be home in a flash." Simone grabbed her purse and rummaged for her keys.

"No worries. We can manage just fine...and tell Nate I hope he enjoys those cinnamon rolls." He gave her a sly wink.

A sheepish look came over her face. "Anna wasn't supposed to tell."

Charlie couldn't help smiling at this little subterfuge arranged by the two sisters. After Nate's last surgery, he'd finally been given the green light to eat solid foods, so Anna had volunteered to babysit while Simone smuggled homemade cinnamon rolls into Nate's hospital room.

So Charlie had volunteered to babysit the babysitter.

He had nefarious plans of his own.

Simone tiptoed up and gave Charlie a quick peck on the cheek. "Thanks for helping Anna with Bobby."

"It's my pleasure, believe me."

"I'm sure it is." Simone tossed her hair back and smiled knowingly, and then her brow drew down, and her expression altered. "How did your conversation with the prosecutor go today?"

"Pretty well, I suppose." Sheriff Hawkins had survived a bullet to the chest courtesy of a Kevlar vest. Charlie had taken the prosecutor, an old friend, to lunch in exchange for an update on the case. "With our testimony, and Nate's of course, the state has all they need to nail Hawkins for attempted murder." He hesitated.

"But?"

"But the prosecutor didn't think the case against Hawkins for the murder of Catherine Timmons was a sure thing—mostly circumstantial. So they offered Hawkins a deal: in exchange for a full confession, they took the death penalty off the table."

"And Hawkins confessed to Catherine's murder?"

Charlie nodded. "Apparently, she'd been digging around in Hawkins's finances and asking questions about the gunshot residue on Megan's hands. Hawkins panicked. If it came out that he'd tampered with evidence, that he'd covered up Megan's murder in exchange for a bribe, he stood to lose everything."

"Tampered with evidence, how?"

"It's complicated."

The look on Simone's face had him hanging his head. Her world had been turned upside down. Her own life had been threatened, and her husband still lay in a hospital bed recovering from near fatal injuries. If she wanted details, he owed them to her. "The night Megan died, Hawkins took two different gunshot residue samples: one for a quick on-the-scene test and another to send out to the crime lab. The BlueView, that's the rapid test, showed no nitrates present on Megan's hands, despite the fact she was still holding the gun that killed her."

"I don't understand."

"Caleb shot Megan, then wiped the gun clean to remove his prints before planting it in her hand. That's why the rapid test showed no nitrates. No nitrates, therefore no gunpowder. Hawkins realized right away that Megan didn't shoot herself. After questioning Megan's mother, he went straight to the Carlisle home, looking for Nate."

"Only Caleb intervened." She put her palm to her forehead.

"That's right. Caleb bribed Hawkins to help expedite a suicide ruling. So Hawkins fired his own gun, then simply took a gunshot residue sample from his own hand and switched it with the one that had been earmarked for the crime lab."

"I think I see. But if the two tests showed different results..." Simone drew her bottom lip between her teeth in a mannerism that made him think of Anna.

Then again, almost every thing these days made him think of Anna. "The crime lab looks at the sample under an electron microscope. Those results are far more accurate than a quick chemical test, so the rapid test was simply dismissed as sampling error."

Simone looked away, her posture sagging, her mood more serious than a few moments ago when all her thoughts had been focused on sneaking cinnamon rolls into the hospital. "I'm so sorry, Drex."

"Hey." He softened his voice. "You've got nothing to be sorry for."

Her back straightened. "But Nate does, and I'm his wife. Did you know Nate sent five hundred dollars every two weeks to Mrs. O'Neal—for years?"

"After everything came out, I suspected it was him."

"Nate told me he was so ashamed of what happened between him and Megan, he couldn't bear for us—for you and me, Drex—to know the truth." She located a Kleenex in her purse and dabbed her eyes. "So he sent Megan's mother money, knowing she wouldn't tell, and he kept on sending her money until Bobby was born. He said after his son was born, he couldn't bear to look at me and keep on lying, so he just stopped sending the money and waited for the chips to fall."

Charlie offered Simone his hand. "Nate's not perfect, Simone. None of us are."

"I love my husband, Drex." She held her head high. "I just wish we could've trusted each other sooner." Then she squeezed his hand and walked through the door.

∼

CHARLIE INHALED A sweet breath of honeysuckle evening, and a warm feeling spread through his chest like a widening smile. It was good to be sitting on a porch swing, watching fireflies race across the summer sky. It was even better to be sitting on that swing, watching the firefly derby with Anna. They'd finally gotten Bobby to sleep, and with the little guy tucked in safely, Charlie knew this was his moment.

"I've been thinking it over, Anna," he said without preliminary. "And I've decided to postpone med school for a year. I've decided to stay here, in Tangleheart...with you." His pulse changed rhythms, losing its beats—like his heart was holding its breath.

Anna propped her wrist-cast on the arm of the porch swing and looked down at her other hand in her lap. "I don't think that's the right thing to do. I don't want you to give up your dream—"

He grabbed her good hand. "*You're* my dream, Peaches. Besides, I'd only be delaying school for a year."

She shook her head.

But he was undaunted. There was always Plan B: a wooden

crate, filled with peaches, he'd brought with him from the farmers' market.

Reaching inside, he picked out a choice specimen: soft—but not too soft—plump and luscious with a gentle hint of fuzz that tickled his nose when he tested its fresh aroma. *Yes sir, this was one perfect, Tangleheart peach, all right.* "I've got something for you, Anna."

He offered her his hand-selected prize.

"No thanks." She shook her hair, and fireflies swarmed above her head like an electric tiara.

The night air hung hot and still around them, as if it, too, were in a state of limbo. He snuggled the fruit back in the crate. *Back to Plan A?* "Can we talk about this, before you shut me down? I know you don't want me to make a sacrifice, but I don't look at it that way. I've already gotten permission from the dean of admissions and—"

"Geography is not the problem, Charlie. Austin's only a few hours away, and besides, I'm not planning on staying in Tangleheart forever. Of course, I can't leave right now, not when Simone needs me so much, and not until I've got Daddy squared away with his new nurse." Her throat worked in a long swallow. "But I checked out the library school at UT, and Charlie, it looks exciting."

He could hardly believe his luck. He hadn't needed the peaches after all. He leaned forward, eager for her next words.

"But..."

No. No. No. *But* was not an option. Her vanilla scent came to him on a breeze, calling up a near holographic memory of her body moving on top of him. He traced his thumb along the soft underside of her forearm.

"But I just don't know. After six years without a word from you, I thought I'd never see you again—and it nearly killed me getting over you. It's been so long..." Her voice trailed off and her head dropped.

He didn't have his charm gun on him, but he did have that crate of peaches. He tucked his index finger between her chin and her chest and nudged her face up until her gaze met his. "We don't have to decide all the details tonight."

Her eyes glistened in the starlight.

He turned her hand over and pressed a soft kiss into her palm. "Let's just sit out here on the front porch and enjoy this beautiful summer night. Like the old days...remember?"

Brushing her hair off her forehead, she gave him a tight smile. "Sounds good."

Pulling a new specimen from his treasure trove, he coaxed her. "How about a bite?"

Her nose scrunched up, and she turned her face away. "You forget I hate peaches."

"No," he countered. "You forget you love peaches."

Seconds ticked by. He waited. Tried to tempt her by wafting the fragrant fruit beneath her nose, and then waited some more.

Finally, she said, "It's true. I used to love peaches...but now I don't."

Detecting uncertainty in her voice, his chest expanded with fresh hope. He could work with an opening like that. In fact, Anna was headed right where he wanted her to go. Stopping by the farmers' market on the way over had been a stroke of pure genius. "It's because of that worm, isn't it?"

Her brow lifted. "I can't believe you remember."

He pressed his unspoiled peach into her hand.

"No thank you," she said firmly, setting it back in the crate.

He held up his hand. "Just hear me out."

"I don't want a peach, Charlie."

"Anna, listen to me. You love peaches. You always have." Leaning toward her, he mentally prepared his case. "I'm not making this up on my own. I've watched you dance when the season turns, and the first peaches hit the farmers' stands. I've seen you feed your dinner to the dog, just to get to the peach pie at the end of the meal quicker. I've even seen you lick peach juice off your chin at a church social."

"Okay, okay, I admit it." She fiddled with the hem of her shirt. "I *used* to love peaches. That's exactly what I just said. But ever since I bit into a bad one and found half a grody worm hanging out of it, I *stopped* loving peaches."

Her mouth twisted into a defiant pink pucker.

She was putty in his hands. "Anna, there isn't a single worm in any of these peaches. I checked every one in this box. You're turning your nose up at something wonderful based on a wrong assumption. You love peaches. You always have. It's *worms* you hate."

That beautiful smile of Anna's—the one that lit his world like a million fireflies on a thousand summer nights—appeared.

"My stars, Charlie, do you have some sort of point to this whole peach de résistance campaign?"

So that she could feel the truth of his words, he took her hand and placed it against his pounding heart. "I love you, Anna. I always have, and I want a chance to earn back your trust. I want a chance to prove that no matter how sad and terrible the world around us becomes, I won't run away from you again. You loved me once, Anna. You told me so yourself. All you have to do is remember."

She pulled her hand away.

His throat tightened. He was beginning to lose hope again... but then, thank God, she tugged his hand to her own racing heart and tilted her face up invitingly.

He brushed his lips over hers, and she opened eagerly for him.

The kiss was long and sweet and tender—everything a kiss should be when you're with the woman you love.

He could've kissed her like that forever, and he did pull her back for more when she tried to break away, but in the end she gave him a little shove and had her way. Apparently, Anna wanted to be heard, too.

Reaching into the crate, she said, "Thanks for reminding me. As a matter of fact, I do love peaches." Her eyes lifted to meet his. "And I love you, Charlie. So if it's another chance you're after, I gotta admit I'm all for it."

And then Anna Kincaid, the girl of Charlie Drexler's dreams, laughed out loud and took a big fearless bite of a perfect Tangleheart peach.

ENJOY THIS BOOK?

You can make a big difference.

Word of mouth is crucial for any author to succeed. Reviews are the most powerful tools in my arsenal when it comes to getting attention for my books. If you've enjoyed this story, I would be very grateful if you could leave a review. A line or two is all that is needed to make a big difference.

Please click here to leave a review.

Print readers please go to your favorite online retailer and leave a review.

Thank you very much.

HAVE YOU READ THEM ALL?

Thrillers:

The Cassidy & Spenser mystery-thriller series:

COUNTDOWN

STOLEN

NOTORIOUS

FALLEN

JUDGMENT

The Blood Secrets series:

CONFESSION

FIRST DO NO EVIL

Stand Alones:

HUSH
 (A Romantic Suspense Novella)

BE THE FIRST TO KNOW!

I hope you'll join my mailing list. Building a relationship with my readers is the best thing about being a writer. I love to hear from readers, and I occasionally send newsletters with details on new releases, special offers, free book giveaways, or important news.

Sign up for my newsletter here.

Print readers sign up for my newsletter on my website at www.CareyBaldwin.com.

Thank you!

ACKNOWLEDGMENTS

THANK YOU, READERS! You are the reason I write.

I am deeply grateful to my family—Bill, Shannon, Erik, and Sarah—for their love and support. My heartfelt thanks go out to the Kiss and Thrill ladies: Lena, Rachel, Manda, Sarah, Diana, Sharon, Krista, and Gwen for their relentless encouragement, support, and wisdom. And last but never ever least: Courtney, Leigh, and Tessa—your shining examples inspire me, and your friendship lifts me up every day.

Hush: © 2013, © 2017 by Carey Baldwin

All rights reserved.

No part of this book may be reproduced in any form or by any electronic or mechanical means, including information storage and retrieval systems, without written permission from the author, except for the use of brief quotations in a book review.

This is a work of fiction. Names, characters, places, and incidents are the product of the author's imagination or are used fictitiously. Any resemblance to actual events, locales, or persons, living or dead, is purely coincidental.

Countdown: © 2017 by Carey Baldwin; Published by Witness Impulse an imprint of HarperCollins

All rights reserved.

No part of this book may be reproduced in any form or by any electronic or mechanical means, including information storage and retrieval systems, without written permission from the author, except for the use of brief quotations in a book review.

This is a work of fiction. Names, characters, places, and incidents are the product of the author's imagination or are used fictitiously. Any resemblance to actual events, locales, or persons, living or dead, is purely coincidental.

Stolen: © 2017 by Carey Baldwin; Published by Witness Impulse an imprint of HarperCollins

All rights reserved.

No part of this book may be reproduced in any form or by any electronic or mechanical means, including information storage and retrieval systems, without written permission from the author, except for the use of brief quotations in a book review.

This is a work of fiction. Names, characters, places, and incidents are the product of the author's imagination or are used fictitiously. Any resemblance to actual events, locales, or persons, living or dead, is purely coincidental.

First Do No Evil: © 2017 by Carey Baldwin; Published by Lowman Press

All rights reserved.

No part of this book may be reproduced in any form or by any electronic or mechanical means, including information storage and retrieval systems, without written permission from the author, except for the use of brief quotations in a book review.

This is a work of fiction. Names, characters, places, and incidents are the product of the author's imagination or are used fictitiously. Any resemblance to actual events, locales, or persons, living or dead, is purely coincidental.

HUSH:

ISBN: 978-0-9896720-0-9